ROGER PRICE'S

THE

TOMORROW PEOPLE

THE LAST ONE

Gary Russell

The Tomorrow People:
The Last One
Written by Gary Russell
Published in 2025 by
Oak Tree Books
oaktreebooks.uk

in association with
Chinbeard Books

Editor: Paul Simpson
Commissioning/Sub-Editor: Barnaby Eaton-Jones

Cover artwork: Robert Hammond

Gary Russell

The Tomorrow People

in

THE LAST ONE

A Chinbeard Books / Oak Tree Books Original

Contents

The Tomorrow People

If you've never met the Tomorrow People before…

Their names are Adam Newman, Ami Jackson, Marmaduke 'Megabyte' Damon, Kevin Wilson, Lisa Davis and Jade Weston. They seem to be just ordinary teenagers. A bit quieter than most, perhaps. They are not from a distant future, they live on Earth, here and now. They are The Tomorrow People, forerunners of a new race—*homo superior* or even *homo novus*, which is why they are reasonably young. They are nature's response to man's aggression: a new species, wiser and more peace-loving than *homo sapiens*, for they cannot kill. They have gained remarkable powers: they can talk to each other by thought waves—telepathy. They can heal small injuries just by willing it. And they can think themselves from place to place as well—

teleportation. Until more of their race evolve, these teens have responsibility for the future of planet Earth, under the guidance of their mysterious, living Ship that lies beneath the surface of an unnamed island somewhere in the South Pacific Ocean. Even they aren't entirely sure where it is but nor do they worry, because it doesn't really matter. They come and go as they please by teleporting and use the Ship as a base where the Tomorrow People can meet, work, play and even sleep and eat. The Tomorrow People also have friends that aren't part of their new evolution, ordinary humans like Megabyte's father, General Bill Damon, or Ami's mum Hasana or Kevin's Aunt Ruth. They are always ready to help the Tomorrow People in whatever purely human way they can.

With thanks to Roger Price & Brian Finch and Lee Pressman & Grant Cathro.

THE
TOMORROW
PEOPLE
THE LAST ONE

Cold Opening

FOUR YEARS AGO…

Standing on Avoca Beach, looking out at the Pacific Ocean, Adam watched the waves crash against the sand that, a few hours earlier, had been rammed with surfers, eager to catch the morning breaks. However, mostly today, they'd just been served ankle slappers. Adam had seen them from the balcony outside Mart's apartment opposite. He was tempted to go join them—Adam didn't often get the chance to surf up here, on the Central Coast—but he knew it wouldn't have been appropriate.

Not today.

Here he was, stood by himself, thinking… thinking what exactly?

Mart had walked away, finally, about ten minutes ago.

1

"You need time, mate," he had said. "Time to think. Take all you want, I'll be upstairs getting the food ready."

Mart had been Dad's business partner. Adam wasn't entirely sure what the business was exactly, but it had provided both of them with a fair bit of money, which had in turn meant Adam was well-looked after, fed and schooled way down in Manly.

As Adam stood there, staring into the distance, it occurred to him that he knew precious little about his father. Sure, he knew that Dad and Mum had met when they were teenagers in England, and Adam had come along very soon afterwards, before they'd gotten married. Adam was thirteen now, but he wasn't stupid. He knew he hadn't been planned, that his parents were barely eighteen-years-old, if that, although he never doubted that he was wanted and loved by them both.

They had come to Australia when Adam had been two years old and Dad had gone into partnership with Mart doing… whatever it was they did. Mum, however, had met someone else and BANG she was out of their lives. Adam had seen his mum a few times since, but she never seemed enormously interested in him. No, that wasn't fair, because she was always there if he needed her, but it was more a case that she never sought *him* out. Adam always did the chasing.

His Dad hadn't minded, he relished bringing Adam up alone—he'd certainly not remarried. In fact, Adam couldn't remember him even having a girlfriend. It was all work or Adam. Which was nice—Dad always said there was a bond between them. "You'll find out once I'm gone," Dad had joked once. "Don't say that," Adam had replied. "You can't go anywhere."

But Dad had. It started with a recurring cough about a year ago and 'metastasized' (Adam had to look that up in the school library; he didn't like what he found) rapidly.

A month back it was "Don't worry, I'll be fine. Let's just say I used up a lot of my life when I was young and maybe this is life's way of paying me back."

Three days after that it was a flat tone from an ECG machine at the hospital and Mart having to become Adam's temporary guardian until Mum could be found. So far, she'd not resurfaced anywhere or returned any of Mart's calls. She probably didn't even know her ex-husband was dead.

Dead.

What a final word.

Adam wanted to cry, he really did. But he hadn't. Not once. He'd faced this abrupt life-change with… well, he didn't know. But Sean and Ben, the identical 'twins of doom' at school, had said something like "don't sweat it, dude. It'll hit you eventually," which seemed remarkably grown-up from two normally remarkably un-grown-up lads. And Ms Curtis, his teacher, had tried to explain the way grief worked, or didn't, for different people and that it was okay to cry.

All of which seemed unreal, like it was all being said to other people at the time, not really him.

But here, today, ten minutes after Dad's ashes had been tossed into the surf at this very specific point on the beach (Dad had left Mart with very detailed notes about that, which Mart was confused by: "He left exact coordinates and even a map of the beach" he'd said yesterday), Adam still couldn't cry.

He just stared, trying to see if he could still spot any of the ashes, any final sight of Joshua Newman, 1959–1991, who Adam loved with every fibre of his being and who he was never going to see again.

Or hear.

Or hug.

Or…

"I'm terribly sorry," said a man beside him. "It is Adam, isn't it?"

Adam looked up. The man was English going by the accent, in his late thirties probably. Dark hair, a smile, unthreatening.

Unthreatening. That was a strange way to describe anyone, but it was a word that popped straight into Adam's head as he looked at the Englishman.

"How did you know Dad?" Adam asked.

"How do you know I *did*?"

"Because you know my name and you look like the kind of guy he might know. Have known."

The stranger gave a smile. "There's a lot of Josh Newman in you then," he said. "I knew him about twenty years ago, a couple of years before you were born. Haven't seen much of him since." The stranger paused, then added, "He was a good person." Adam thought that was an odd thing to say, or at least an odd way to phrase it, but he appreciated the thought behind it.

"I'm sorry," the stranger said, passing Adam a small business card.

Except it wasn't actually a business one at all. Just a white square with a name on one side, and on the reverse, an image that Adam recognised as being a London Underground logo, red circle, blue bar across it but no station name. He flipped the card back over and again looked at the name.

John Dixon.

Meant nothing to him.

"If ever you find yourself unexpectedly in London, find me," said Mr Dixon.

"How?" asked Adam, and not adding out loud the "And why?" that had formed in his mind.

Mr Dixon flipped the card again, then tapped the Underground symbol. "You'll know." He then started to walk away, although not before throwing a look, as Adam had, in the general direction of wherever the ashes had gone. "I wonder why he wanted this exact time," Mr Dixon muttered, more to himself than to Adam. "Oh, and why should you want to find me?" he added, smiling at Adam again. "The fact that I know that was the question in your head is a clue."

Adam just stared at him. People couldn't read minds, and anyway, it was a perfectly obvious question that anyone might have asked. Or thought about.

Mr Dixon smiled, then walked off, with the gait of a man not used to walking in thick sand, back towards the Avoca Beach car park. He disappeared from view behind the lifeguard hut and bushes between the sand and tarmac.

Adam started to turn back to the sea when something caught his eye. Peripheral vision, they called it.

He swore there were five figures standing watching him, where the beach headed southwards, towards the little cinema.

In his head he immediately clocked them. An elderly woman with greying hair. Another woman, big smiley face, tubby, wearing a dress that wouldn't have been out of place in a pie shop from fifty years ago. The three men were the strangest, though. One was exceptionally tall, but wearing a schoolboy uniform, like out of a comic or an old book. He even held a huge circular lolly. Then there was a... wider man, in a grey T-shirt, red braces and a pork pie hat—the oddest thing about him was that he had a dog leash in his hand, but instead of a dog on the end, there was a tortoise, slowly making its way across the sand. Stranger still was the man at the back of this group, wrapped from head to foot in a red sou'wester and hat, like he'd come in from a fishing trawler at the height of the rainy season.

Adam blinked and as he tried to focus on this weird group, they... now they just weren't there at all. And no one was walking away ether. Had he imagined them? Had there been a tortoise on a leash? Why? Was this some side-effect of the grief he was annoyed with himself for not feeling?

That was bloody weird. People couldn't just appear and disappear. And certainly not dressed up like that!

Adam thought of heading back up to Mart's apartment. All the people that had come for the send-off would be up there, waiting for him. He didn't want to go of course, for two reasons. Firstly, he barely knew them, and he really didn't want to listen to small talk about Dad. And secondly, every moment he stayed on the beach, staring out at that water, trying to see the ashes, he was still connected to Dad. Somehow Dad was still there.

That question still nagged at the back of his mind. Both Mart and that Mr Dixon guy had asked it.

Why was Dad so specific about where and when the ashes had to be let go on this beach?

Adam screwed his eyes up, focussing on the horizon, and wondered what was out there, dozens of kay-emms out in the middle of the ocean, the middle of nowhere.

Suddenly, out of nowhere, Adam had the most powerful and painful headache, like someone had just whacked him with a shovel right on the top of his skull.

If he wanted to yell out in pain, he didn't have a chance because a split-second later, Adam was underwater, soaked, splashing around.

How? What? Why? Where?

Don't drown, he told himself. No matter how shocking this was, don't drown. Push up. Up, break the water. Get air.

He did.

He certainly wasn't on Avoca Beach anymore. Had a tidal wave or tsunami suddenly hit, washed the whole of this part of New South Wales away?

There was land, maybe thirty or forty metres away. Adam was a strong swimmer—he was a surfer, he had to be—so swimming towards it wasn't an issue.

Where it had come from, why he was in the water in the first place, and what the hell was going on today, those were the issues.

After a few moments, Adam dragged himself out of the water onto a warm sandy beach. It was an island, he realised that, but it certainly wasn't the Central Coast of New South Wales after a tidal wave. The trees, the bushes, that told him he wasn't even in Australia any longer.

There was a voice in his head now, and not a headache. No, not a voice, just… sounds, noises, but a rhythm to them. Whatever it was, it seemed to be aimed at him, it seemed almost—and this was just stupid—but yeah, it seemed to be calling to him in words and sounds he'd never heard before.

Adam walked up the beach, focussing in on the sounds inside his head.

A word did form in his mind, not spoken by these strange noises, but it was like his brain was trying to translate the sounds.

Ship.

Adam kept walking forwards.

Ship.

He needed to find a ship?

Why did he need to find a ship?

And the rest, as they say, was history.

Episode One

NOW...

"Happy birthday, Adam!"

Adam winced slightly at both the noise and general exuberance echoing around the Ship. Well, that and the fact that generally birthdays and other personal celebrations weren't really his thing.

Megabyte suddenly grabbed his shoulders from behind and planted a big sarcastic kiss on the back of his head. "Happy birthday, boss," he laughed.

Jade was more gentle and slightly more genuine as she kissed his cheek. "Happy seventeenth, Adam. You don't look a day over twenty-one."

Kevin ran up and grabbed his hand, shaking it over-enthusiastically—but then over-enthusiasm was very much Kevin's schtick. "Congratulations, Adam. You survived another year of Megabyte and

Ami dogging your every move while Lisa and I went exploring the world."

Lisa coughed loudly. "I think you'll find I explored and all you did was try out every café and candy store that sold milkshakes." She smiled at Adam. "Honestly, he found flavours no one knew existed."

"And if they didn't," Kevin continued, "I got them to invent new ones based on the local fruits." He stopped. "I have to say, there was something I had on Cozumel, from a little shack on the beach there that did not agree with me."

"Bubblegum and mamey sapote," Lisa filled in the details. "The colour of his sick was very exciting. And amusing."

Ami stepped forward, ever the adult. She had a small box covered in birthday wrapping paper which she silently handed to Adam, who took it with all the practised expertise of someone utterly unused to receiving gifts and knowing what to say in return. "Thank you," he managed quietly, his face breaking into a grin. "I wasn't expecting… anything."

"It's from all of us," Kevin said.

Jade, Lisa and Ami nodded.

"Except it isn't really," Kevin added, tactful as always. "I mean we all meant to contribute, and we probably will, but really it was chosen by Megabyte cos he was the one who knew it was today. Your birthday I mean. Today."

As the others all threw Kevin the glare that they always reserved for his always well-meaning, but frequently inappropriate, comments, Adam—however—caught Megabyte's eye and nodded a slight thank you.

Megabyte grinned like someone had just given him a million dollars and said, "Ami wrapped it cos, you know, these fingers can't do anything well." He waved his hands around to demonstrate.

Adam unwrapped the box and took a deep intake of breath.

It was a photograph. In a silver, and very expensive looking, frame.

The photo showed a shortish, thin man with jet black hair and a huge happy grin, standing in some trees, a waterfall behind them. He was holding the hand of a young boy, aged maybe seven, in big beach shorts. The boy was looking up at the man, utter admiration and adoration in his young eyes.

Adam stared and stared. Finally he managed to say "How… Where did… I mean…"

After that, he had no words.

Sensing this might be get awkward, Megabyte

jumped in. "Taken ten years ago today, on your seventh birthday. In Ku-ring-gai—hope I said that right." He leaned over and nudged Adam's shoulder with his own. "You can thank some guy called Uncle Mart, who my dad managed to track down in some primitive outpost near Sydney."

Ami stood behind Adam and rested her chin on his other shoulder.

"Is that you? Oh my god, you were a-dork-able!"

Jade, Lisa and Kevin gathered round too. "Who he?" Jade asked.

No one other than Ami noticed the tiny look that shot between Adam and Megabyte.

"He's… he was my Dad," Adam said. "Joshua Newman." He took a deep breath. "He died on my thirteenth birthday."

If anyone knew how to break the awkward silence that followed, they chose not to do so.

"It's okay, guys," Adam said. "I got over it, a long time ago." He stared at the photo again. "But I think this is the only photo I have of him, and I had no idea it existed. Thank you. All of you."

Almost too quickly, the rest of the Tomorrow People gathered there found something else to talk about, being teenagers and utterly incapable of dealing with emotions and things like that.

Except Ami.

Just as Adam had been appointed leader of the Tomorrow People, not by his choice but by design, respect and admiration, so Ami had become the 'mum' of the group, despite her young age. She was first to sort out any squabbles, she was the first to seek out first aid if anyone was hurt, she was the first anyone went to with a problem.

And she was the first Adam always turned to.

"It's an amazing thing," he said to her, finally.

"He must have been an amazing man," she replied.

Adam nodded. "Without him... well, let's just say I learned everything *from* him."

Ami leaned in and kissed him again, this time on the nose. "Megabyte did a lot of research to find that."

Adam grinned. "I suspect General Damon did," he said, meaning Megabyte's powerful and well-connected Dad.

Ami shook her head. "Nope, all his own work. Which, I might add, was harder than he expected."

"Why's that? Its only Australia, not Mars."

"Because someone, no prizes for guessing who, just watch my eyes..." and Ami stared Adam straight in the face. "Someone is very secretive

15

about their background. You, Mr Newman, know all our families. Mums, dads, brothers and sisters, even mad old aunts. But we know nothing of *yours*. We had no idea if your parents were alive or dead, whether there was any family at all out there. He went to a lot of effort."

Adam grinned. "Sorry. I don't mean to be ultra-private, I just… am, I guess."

Ami grinned back. "We kinda noticed."

"So, why'd he go to all that effort? Not that I'm ungrateful, but I'd've thought he'd have better things to do than worry about my Dad."

Ami sighed. "Sometimes you are the most dazzling, gorgeous, powerful person I know, Adam," she said. "And sometimes, you're a complete moron who can't see anything even when it's standing right in front of him. Now, I'm going to get a can of cola. Want one?"

Without waiting for a reply, Ami popped over to the far side of the Ship, leaving Adam perplexed by her comments.

But then, he frequently was.

The Damons' divorce was final, then. The papers that had just been faxed over to the house confirmed that.

Christina was staying in Boston and Millie was staying with her, leaving Marmaduke with him here in London. The Service would pay for the big house here, and probably for the Boston place so Christina would be okay there. Then it was just going to be endless flights back and forth to see his daughter or for Christina to come here and see their son—it was going to get messy. Plus there was the matter that he needed to sit and talk to Marmaduke about it—not a conversation he was looking forward to.

Sure, the boy knew things had been rocky ever since they'd moved to the UK, oh six years ago, but he knew very little about exactly how bad it was. Why should he have all that inflicted on him? He was still at college (allegedly—there were times that that may not have been entirely true. Or provable) and deserved to have his teenage years unburdened by his father's domestic problems.

General Bill Damon's thoughts were interrupted by the doorbell ringing.

Once, a few years back, the Service supplied a guy to do things like answer the door. Of course, that same guy was also there to put himself in front of a bullet if someone tried to take General Damon out. But as his work had changed and adapted, so the Service no longer thought he was in danger.

This was good, for both General Damon and Marmaduke.

It did mean, he noted wryly to himself, that he now had to answer his own front door.

"Hi," he said with his usual dazzling smile that he tended to keep for newbies at work, to put them at their ease. But the lady on his doorstep didn't look like she needed that particular smile.

Mainly because she was giving him exactly the same one. "Bill Damon? The General? How lovely to finally meet you."

"I'm sorry, should I…?"

"Oh absolutely not," she said. "You've never heard of me. My name is Letitia de Lillevilt-O'lidam. I'm a vet to exotic animals. Everyone calls me Lottie Oldham. Perhaps you've seen my posters on the trees, lampposts and even in the Post Office window?"

General Bill Damon was rarely thrown by strangers, it was in his training to think on his feet and react in a split-second. Peoples' lives often depended on it. However Lottie Oldham's demeanour and unflinching smile utterly threw him.

"I'm sorry," he stammered. "We don't have pets."

"Oh I know, I know," Lottie said, neatly stepping past him and into the large hall of the massive London house he was living in, as if she owned it. Or had at least been invited in a dozen times before. "But you really should. And yes, a cup of tea would be delicious, thank you, Bill."

General Damon realised for the first time that she was dragging along a rather large canvas shopping trolley on wheels. She dragged it over the threshold, and his only thought was he hoped the wheels didn't damage the flooring. He still hoped to get his deposit back when the lease was up on this place.

The old lady, Lottie, patted her trolley. "There, there dear," she seemed to be saying to something inside. "Not long now."

General Damon was now beyond bewildered by the odd turn his morning had taken. He was now downright confused.

He was also suspicious. Over the last few years he'd seen and dealt with a number of extraordinary situations, people, and at one point utterly alien, that 99.9% of mankind would never know about.

The hairs on the back of his hand tickled. Lottie Oldham triggered that small part of his mind that was forever expecting the next invasion from Mars or supernatural visitor or—

"Coffee is fine, if you don't have tea," Lottie said, striding towards the kitchen, still dragging her trolley behind her. "I know you American types don't really like tea much, do you?"

"Now look, madam," General Damon started but Lottie Oldham reached out and patted the back of his hand and shook her head.

"Don't get upset, General." She patted the trolley again. "We won't disturb you for long, will we, my beautiful baby?"

If General Damon was going to reply to that, he didn't. Because suddenly he was flailing his arms about, trying to reach the door handle, or a stair banister rail or anything that would steady him. It was as if someone had anaesthetised his legs out from under him and before he could even gasp, he was on the floor, at eye level with some kind of octopus-like creature, the exact kind of which he'd never seen before.

Then as he watched, unable to move, the creature seemed to grow larger and larger as the hallway around him became darker and darker...

General Damon found he could move, get up again. He scrabbled to his feet, trying to work out where he was. It was just… darkness. A darkened room, he somehow knew it was huge, endless, and he began running because tentacles the size of elephant trunks and still growing, were reaching towards his retreating body.

He could hear them flopping and squishing against the floor, the walls, the ceilings… He could now smell some really quite fetid breath from the creature, and feel the air around him wobble and waft as the tentacles thrashed around, reaching for his ankles.

He ran and ran and ran and ran and…

There was a hole. He only knew this because he fell into it and didn't stop falling, looking up, as he dropped, into the face of the old laughing woman that grew larger and larger no matter how far he fell.

Mr Jones was a busy man; he had little time for fun or jokes or mystery. And don't get him started on the state of British television or films or that interweb thing everyone was talking about.

Right now, he was late for work; the queue at the sandwich shop had been far too long and his lunch hour was almost up. Quite when he was going to eat his ham and piccalilli sandwich, he didn't know. It was frowned upon in the office to eat at his desk, but that was his only option.

Or he stood on the corner and ate it in in the street. Which was unpleasant and common. Not to say anything of the possible indigestion side-effects that would follow.

Luckily there wasn't another soul for, well, anywhere. And he could see in both directions up the long High Street. No one would know. Wait, a bus had turned in. All those people on the top deck would indeed see him if he opened his sandwich.

Bother.

As he stood there, on the kerb by the zebra crossing, waiting for the bus to get down the High Street so he could cross safely (no risk taking for him), his eye drifted to the Mission House. A tall red brick place that was a gathering place for the elderly and infirm. Mostly old women, of an age and era that they'd probably never worked and thus earned pensions. Oh, a couple had probably done something during the war or operated telephones in the exchange, but most had never done more than char around their own houses.

Mr Jones thought that was wise. His office

was overrun by women these days. The boss, Mr MacKintosh, said they made the place more efficient and better organised and were harder workers. Mr Jones took exception to that, thought that untrue and suspected Mr MacKintosh had been watching too much television or films or been using the interwebs. See, the world was falling apart.

The bus was just blocking his view of the Mission House when he heard a noise, like electrical energy.

He jumped. Was some stupid telegraph pole going to fall on his head, electrocuting him?

Apparently not, but he could definitely smell the acrid after-aroma of electrical current. It was in the air; he could taste it as well, just on the corners of his mouth. Like when, as a child, he'd licked a nine volt battery in a dare with Tommy Smith.

As the bus moved on, there was a lad standing outside the Mission.

How had he got there? That was impossible, the road had been empty, and the bus hadn't stopped. So where did he come from.

The teen saw him and, good lord, he waved at Mr Jones. What cheek. Young people today, no manners or decorum.

The boy turned and walked up the steps into the Mission House.

Well, hopefully someone in there would teach him some manners.

"Outrageous behaviour, isn't it," said a woman's voice beside him.

Where no one had been standing a moment before.

"Youngsters," she said.

"Absolutely," Mr Jones found himself nodding with the old lady he'd never seen before.

From behind her, the old lady swung round a canvas shopping trolley, the sort Mr Jones always saw people of a certain vintage dragging behind them.

He flinched. He didn't like this woman for some reason. She had an air about her...

The old lady frowned. "You've nothing to fear from me," she muttered.

Mr Jones hadn't said anything. How did she know...

"Although perhaps the sort of man who eats piccalilli with ham, doesn't appreciate women in the office *and* is late back to work," she continued, "*should* be alarmed."

Mr Jones had had enough and decided to ignore her and her stupid trolley.

He stepped out onto the zebra crossing as the road was clear.

Mr Jones wasn't on a zebra crossing.

He was on a rope bridge, his hands gripping at the rope while the loose planks beneath his feet wobbled dangerously.

And as he looked down, he could see he was two hundred feet above a sheer drop, the tiny river below was barely visible.

How did he get here? This was hot, like a jungle.

The bridge swayed again.

He carefully turned, to step back to safety, but he realised he couldn't see the end of the bridge, just swampy mist.

He turned again, sure enough the other side was lost in mist too.

But this was impossible, he decided. One minute he'd been on the High Street with that old woman and some rude teenager, and now he was... somewhere in Africa. Or South America.

Trapped on a swaying rope bridge with loose wooden slats and too scared to step one way or the other.

Worse still, his ham and piccalilli sandwich was no longer in his pocket...

Adam Newman entered the Mission House through the big wood and glass doors, and was about to close them when he shuddered.

Like someone was walking over his grave.

Which was an odd sensation for a Tomorrow Person because as a rule, they were ultra-sensitive to what was going on around them; it was a side-effect of their powers. Ami had often suggested that maybe their powers were tied in to planet Earth itself—it would certainly explain why some of their individual strengths, like Adam's healing abilities or Ami's telekinesis or Kevin's foresight, tended to fluctuate in strength depending on the weather or seasons.

So, any tingling feeling, any preternatural sense of foreboding shouldn't really happen.

Adam was suddenly convinced he was being watched.

Before shutting the doors, he looked back out onto the High Street, but the only person there was the man by the zebra crossing, the one he'd cheekily waved at just now (Adam knew he'd be flummoxed by Adam's jaunting in), and he was still stood there, looking in the general direction the bus had taken.

It went through Adam's mind that now the road was empty of traffic the man really could have gone across the crossing, but the fact he'd chosen not to was up to him.

Other than that, the road was completely devoid of human beings.

Adam turned back to face the building's interior and let the doors fall closed behind him.

Had he turned back at that moment, he might have seen that the area wasn't empty at all.

Standing with her nose almost pressed up against the glass, which would have been impossible because no one could move that fast, was an old lady with a canvas shopping trolley.

Unless, like Adam, she had jaunted there.

But that was just silly.

Old ladies weren't Tomorrow People.

The local police radios were working overtime that day. Since 10 a.m., various officers on the beat or on panda cars were reporting that they had picked up people doing strange things, often quite dangerously.

The young man who was standing on top of the multi-storey car-park, insisting he was wire-walking between the Leo Burnett Building and the Marina Tower in Chicago. The woman who was sat up a tree in the park, mewling like a kitten, claiming she had been chased up there by a giant spider. The businessman diving behind parked cars, waving a banana and adamant that he'd been involved in a gunfight with Al Capone. There were dozens of others, people all doing peculiar things, but more alarmingly, all utterly convinced they were elsewhere.

The latest one came in at lunchtime, an accountant who was holding up traffic by jumping back and forth on all the white stripes on a zebra crossing, convinced he was on a rope bridge near Machu Picchu. Like everyone else, once his... hysteria had worn off, he couldn't explain why he had behaved that way. Weirder in his case, he was also very angry that some old lady had stolen his ham and piccalilli sandwich.

The police weren't entirely sure what to do other than release everyone without charge, just a warning not to do it again as no one had actually committed any real crime or hurt anyone else.

Unnoticed by anyone, even people who passed her, was an old lady standing outside the Mission House, canvas shopping trolley beside her, noshing on a ham and piccalilli sandwich. She was smiling, thinking about the chaos she had wrought that morning.

"And they still don't know about Bill Damon or Hasana Jackson? Now we visited the Wilson and Weston homes earlier and I'm not yomping over to America for the Davises or the rest of the Damons. Lottie Oldham is far too ancient for that, isn't she my beautiful pet?"

Whatever was inside the shopping trolley burbled in reply.

"Happy birthday, Adam!"

Adam winced slightly at the noise. Again. Just as he had thousands of miles away the day before, in the Ship.

This time, the cheers and congratulations came from the elderly men and women who populated the Mission House on this particular day. Once a week, Adam came here to help serve food and play board games and generally give something to the community.

It had started about a year earlier—Adam's then girlfriend Lucy had been doing community service here; Lucy saw herself as an investigative journalist for the local paper, the authorities saw her as a troublemaker who broke into buildings unlawfully and accessed information unlawfully and generally made a nuisance of herself, usually unlawfully. One day she'd gone too far, got arrested and sentenced to two hundred hours community service, which had led her to the Mission House and its inhabitants.

Adam, always ready to support Lucy, no matter how much trouble she was in, had joined in and found he really enjoyed talking to the old people there.

Maybe it was because having lost his dad, and having no clue where his mum was, it gave him some people from the older generation to talk to, discuss things with, occasionally sort out problems. One of those problems had in fact *been* Lucy whose casual disregard for rules and regulations often conflicted with Adam's own ethics. He had no problem bending said rules, but never really breaking them. Worse still, if he got caught, he would take his punishment. Lucy rebelled against it, seeing everything as an attack on her and her 'freedom of the press' stance. And although that devil-may-care attitude had been appealing eighteen months ago, it had rapidly worn off and they'd broken up about six months back.

They still saw it each other here occasionally (two hundred hours of community service is a *lot* of community service) but Adam was fully aware that she was now seeing an eco-warrior who squatted on a houseboat in Brentford and smoked a lot of dope. Fine and dandy, but not Adam's thing at all.

"And how is young Ami?" asked Mr Cooper.

"Have you asked her out on a date yet?" added Mrs Ainscott, although she said the word 'date' as if it was a term she'd never dream of using herself. In her young day, it was probably called 'wooing' and 'dates' were something you ate at Christmas with a wooden fork or marked on a calendar.

Adam immediately wanted to be somewhere else. "No," he said truthfully "It's not really the right time."

He desperately wanted to change the subject. If he'd been embarrassed by the birthday cake a few moments earlier, this line of questioning was certainly going to make him even more uncomfortable.

Of course, he adored Ami, and she him. There had been moments when, either eating pizza in Tottenham Court Road or sushi in Minato City, that he'd come close to suggesting a night at the cinema or a walk over the Sydney Harbour Bridge (the great thing about their teleporting powers, world travel was now very cheap) but he sensed that Ami was… holding back? Or something else. He was sure it wasn't complete disinterest but he felt that Ami was forcing herself *not* to get closer, to keep a slight distance between them, but he didn't know why.

Then there had been that weird comment last night about him being a moron who couldn't see what was in front of him. He wondered if she had been talking about herself, but no. Something in her voice suggested it was something else entirely.

But he had no idea what.

The Tomorrow People of course had telepathic powers as part of their repertoire. But they didn't use it much, tending to jaunt in when they needed to speak to one another, and only using their telepathy in dire emergencies—like fighting off ancient Egyptian pharaohs, or alien rocks, or a renegade group of Sorson warriors—and they would never read one another's minds without permission. But Adam had been tempted to sneak into Ami's head more than once. But then rationality and a sense of decency had always taken over.

Maybe he should talk to Jade; her 'additional' power seemed to be low-level empathy, reading moods, and sometimes influencing them. Perhaps she could work out Ami's angle.

His reverie was interrupted by Mr Cooper tugging at the sleeve of Adam's baggy sweater.

"Have you met Lottie?"

Adam looked around, trying to spot the object of Mr Cooper's query. No, he certainly hadn't, if it were the eccentric old lady with the trolley standing by the doorway to the room.

This Lottie lady strode towards him, a huge grin on her face.

Adam took an involuntary step back, but he wasn't sure why.

"Hullo," he said.

"Oh, how adorable," Lottie replied. "Australian, yes?"

Adam nodded. It was all he could do. Whoever this person was, he found her incredibly intimidating, despite her smiles and apparent harmlessness.

"I went to Australia once. Full of spiders and snakes and drop bears. Very unpleasant."

"Drop bears aren't—" Adam started, but Lottie waved his protest away.

"Yes dear boy, I know, I know." She tapped the side of her nose, as if imparting a huge secret. "But all legends and myths have their origins in truth somewhere. There were drop bears once, you know." Then, disconcertingly, she looked Adam straight in the eyes. "I should know, I helped wipe them out."

At which point Adam did something he'd never done before. He jaunted away in full view of a room full of people who had no idea he was a Tomorrow Person.

If Adam could have seen the reaction of the old age pensioners left behind in the Mission House, he would have been somewhat shocked.

None of them had panicked, or fainted, or called the police or even muttered about it.

No, they all just carried on as if teenaged lads vanishing in electrical crackle happened all the time.

Lottie Oldham sniffed the air, drawing in the faint electrical discharge in the ar.

"Well, Adam Newman, that was rather rude."

Lottie looked back at the old people around her. One other thing Adam's disappearance had denied him the chance to see was that the moment he went, everybody's eyes closed. Everyone except Lottie. Behind their eyelids however, their eyes flickered and moved rapidly.

Mr Cooper tapped Lottie's shoulder, clearly still able to see despite his closed eyes. "Lottie dear, have you, you know, done what you set out to do?"

Lottie nodded. "Megabyte's father, both Ami's

and Jade's mothers, all locked away in my little Home for Wayward Parental Units."

"What about dear Adam's relatives?" asked Mrs Ainscott.

Lottie pursed her lips "His father is dead, his mother is long gone too. That only leaves his mad old grannie."

Mr Cooper nodded. "Oh, so where do we find her, dear?"

Mrs Ainscott joined in. "Is she here in London too?"

Lottie Oldham patted the back of both their hands. "Oh, bless you, you poor sweet useless brain-dead example of *homo sapiens*."

Mr Copper and Mrs Ainscott just smiled as if they'd been paid an enormous compliment. But then again, they were completely in Lottie's mental thrall.

"Adam's grannie is right here," Lottie said. "And you're looking at her."

Episode Two

THREE YEARS AGO…

Anderson Lewis House was part of a large estate a few miles north of London, on the Herts border. Over the years it had been a family home, a suite of executive offices for a Saudi office supplies company and most recently a set of small apartments rented for six months at a time by businessmen travelling to the UK from all over the world.

Officially, according to the estate agents charged with selling it at the end of 1992, it had become too monolithic to maintain to a high enough standard for people to want to pay £500 a week to stay there.

Unofficially everyone locally knew that the place was haunted—or even if you didn't believe in ghosts, enough people did—and that was keeping people away.

It had been suggested by more than one local, usually down the Saxon's Head at 10:30 p.m. when a sufficient quantity of whisky had been consumed, that the building needed an exorcism/a séance/burning to the ground/turning into free apartments for the homeless of Watford and Hemel Hempstead.

None of these were taken terribly seriously by the Estate Agents—well, except one. And that wasn't taken seriously so much as seen as a way to garner some interest locally and on the news. Burning it down: looks like insurance fraud. Turning into apartments for the needy: no return for anyone's investments. Exorcism: frowned upon by the church, frankly. But a séance: there was publicity in that and, handled properly, a good sense of fun.

Thus it was that the Estate Agents contacted Myron Hardcastle, a minor celebrity on a couple of burgeoning satellite television channels and, only a few weeks earlier had been a guest on *This Morning with Richard and Judy* (sadly on an episode where the titular stars were on holiday so some Z-list celebs were sat on the famous sofa that morning).

But Myron Hardcastle told ITV's viewers that he would absolutely hold a séance at Anderson Lewis House shortly.

In truth, Myron knew that it wouldn't work.

The house simply didn't have the right vibes about it—there were no ghosts, no ancient spirits to drum up there. So, he held a party at his own house one night, had friends invite random people that he didn't know and he selected three of them to join him in a trial séance at Anderson Lewis House before the official one the press would be covering.

That way, he'd get a real idea of how to spin it for the cameras (maybe Richard and Judy would come along to the real one) and make it look good. Like all good mediums, Myron had rehearsals. It was still a performance, still a show. You *had* to get it right.

He didn't really know the three people sat around the table in the library of Anderson Lewis House that night. All he'd ascertained about them was that they were sceptics, which were always the best. It meant that while they were adamant they *didn't* believe, they absolutely did, deep down. Or at least wanted to believe, and thus would be willing to suspend disbelief and be shocked when Myron performed his set-up tricks and mechanics.

If he could convince them, convincing Richard and Judy (of course they'd come) would be a huge launchpad for the next stage of his television career.

No more 1 a.m. broadcasts to six insomniacs and a cat from Marco Polo House in Battersea—this would see him getting prime time slots, performing live spectaculars on ITV from Liverpool Albert Dock studios. He would be famous.

His trio were all in their late thirties, all party animals and all raring to go. Myron suspected that alcohol, and maybe something else, was very much what was keeping them in such high spirits this evening.

First up was Loz, a rich fop from a wealthy part of London who probably lived on Daddy's money and had a fleet of sports cars, women and fashionable dogs like Salukis or Sloughis. Myron had loathed him the moment he was introduced to him.

Then there were the couple, Charly and Neal. Charly was an alcoholic (you could see it in her face; her skin creases, red cheeks and dark eyes making her look twenty years older than she was) and Neal was her enabler, a tall, balding man who talked endlessly about men he'd beaten up in restaurants and nightclubs for daring to look at the no-doubt drunken Charly.

They sat in the darkened room, round a circular table, holding hands as requested by Myron and focussing on a set of five tarot cards, two candles and a set of upturned glass tumblers on a lace table-cloth.

Charly giggled. Loz sniggered. Neal sighed.

Myron hated them all with each passing second. Appalling human beings, all three. But he needed them. Because they were the kind of people who would talk about what they were about to experience and spread the word, making Myron famous!

Myron began the séance as he always did, whispered foreboding words, a bit of general mumbling and some nonsensical mystic metrics.

He'd got about three minutes into it when everyone shivered as the air turned cold.

Myron thought that was odd as he hadn't brought his air blower with him—the noise rather gave the game away.

Then that wretched Charly woman started spoiling things by muttering and groaning herself, pretending she was presumably in contact with the spirits. He could see Neal and Loz both enjoying her mickey-taking, but frankly it annoyed him. He was about to stop her when things went... a bit awry.

Firstly, Charly stood up, breaking the circle.

She looked straight at Myron. "Thank you," she said. "You have no idea how long I have been waiting for this particular gene-pool to come into this particular room. I mean," she laughed, "the odds were pretty badly stacked against me."

Neal stood up. "Charly…" he began.

"Oh dear boy, Charly doesn't live here anymore," said Charly. "I'm afraid she's gone for good. Which is just as well as the damage she's done to this body is shocking. Shocking I tell you. The world is better off now she's dead."

Neal turned to Myron, fists balling. "Now look, mate, what's going on?"

That was the last time Myron and Loz ever saw Neal. He simply vanished. One second he was in the room, the next, he was gone.

Loz clapped slowly. "Oh well, done, man, that's so brilliant. Mirrors? Curtains?"

Then Loz was gone too.

Myron pressed himself further into his chair. He had no idea what was going on, but he knew this wasn't going to get him a golden-handcuffs deal with ITV.

"I sent the first one back to the time of the Crusades. The other one probably just found himself in the Battle of Ypres. Not sure which one but let's face it, his life expectancy is probably less than thirty seconds. No one'll miss either of them."

"Who are you?" stammered Myron.

"But this one, oh she'll do me very well. Charlotte Dell. Ooh she's gone back to using her maiden name. Well, that marriage was never really going to work out for her."

Myron didn't understand. "But they weren't married…"

"Oh not Neal thingy, no. I mean her actual husband. Her drinking, you see, broke them up years ago. Now I need to find the poor abandoned ex-hubby, and say hullo. Not seen him in about two decades. I'm sure he'll be overjoyed. I certainly will."

"What are you talking about?"

"Still need to get this body in better shape." Before Myron's shocked eyes, Charly's body started to change, to get older until he realised he was looking at a version of Charly that was closer to seventy than thirty-five. "Oh that's better. Toxins all gone, organs had a chance to flush themselves out, although that liver's always going to be an issue." Whoever or whatever Charly was now stared down at Myron Hardcastle. "Now, what shall we do about you? Always had a soft spot for mediums and spiritualists. Not your fault you're too stupid to understand that behind every bit of fakery, there's a smidgeon of truth."

The Estate Agents came back around lunchtime the next day. They found no sign of Lawrence Clements, Neal Lyons or Charlotte Dell. But

Myron Hardcastle was curled up in a ball, sobbing and muttering that he'd seen the First One and that she was going to become the Last One.

No one had the slightest clue what he was jabbering on about.

Anderson Lewis House was demolished six months later, and a housing estate ultimately got built on the land. No one raised any objections.

Myron Hardcastle never got the fame he sought. Indeed, he died two years later in an Institution. He never spoke another coherent sentence in all that time.

NOW...

Inside the Ship, chaos had finally been cleaned up. Adam's birthday party had continued long after the guest of honour himself had jaunted back to London.

Ami was overseeing the clean-up—she was never quite sure at one point it had been decided she was the 'mum' of their gang, but it had happened organically and everyone just accepted her role in their lives. If Ami said "clean", they cleaned. If she said "sort out the bedrooms" they sorted them.

Everyone liked Ami, which was easy to understand, because she was really quite pleasant, honest and charming to everyone. She had adapted to life as a Tomorrow Person very easily (heck, she'd even won her over-protective mum around eventually) and very happily. No matter the dangers, no matter to life-threatening challenges, Ami faced them with a joy and gung-ho attitude the others all admired.

Lisa came up to her and hugged her. "Gotta head home now, Mom will be worrying where we are."

Ami nodded, catching Kevin's eye. "You be good, Kevin Wilson, and take care of Lisa, okay?"

Kevin had been living in the States for a year or so now, enrolled in some college not far from Lisa's home, and their blossoming romance grew stronger and healthier every day.

"Oh and when was the last time you popped over to London and said hi to your own mum and dad?"

Kevin sighed. "I promised them I'd be home for Easter this year, so I'll be back in a few weeks."

Megabyte sauntered over, ruffling Kevin's hair as he did so. "Good to see ya, buddy," he said. "Don't forget to write."

Kevin gave his oldest friend a big hug. After all, their Tomorrow People adventure had started together when they were both schoolfriends, pranking older boys, and getting into trouble for it so many times.

Then Kevin and Lisa were gone in a flash of electricity.

"And then there were three," called Jade, who was polishing the main column of the Ship. "There, all cleaned up. What do you think, Ship?"

The Ship's walls pulsated slightly in greens and yellows, suggesting it was happy, and faint unintelligible burbles could be heard rumbling from deep within the structure's bowels.

"Adam says he can understand what Ship says," Jade said. "I can sense its moods, but I wish I could actually speak to it like he does."

Ami shrugged. "I've never been quite sure if he really can talk to it or its some kind of extension of his healing powers that created a connection with it."

"Maybe it's cos he was first to find it," Megabyte offered.

Jade was staring upwards, towards the chute that exited up and onto the island's beach dozens of metres above them, which in the old days they used to use to get in or out until they fully mastered jaunting to exact coordinates.

"Was he? I mean, this Ship has been here centuries—must have been to be this far under the island. It's like the island grew around it," she said. "Adam was the first of *us*, but I wonder if there were other Tomorrow People over the centuries who lived here."

Megabyte grinned. "Cool," he said. "How can we find out about them? Wonder if old Tutankhamun ever paid the Ship a visit."

Jade shrugged, recalling Ami telling her about their encounter with a Tomorrow Person from ancient times. "Ask Adam?" she said. "I mean, get him to ask the Ship."

"Yeah, if he can really talk to it," Megabyte agreed.

Jade shrugged. "Meanwhile, are we waiting for him to come back, or all going home now?"

Ami slipped her hand into Megabyte's, much to his surprise.

Jade's too. "Okay, well I'm, off anyway. See you all soon." She tapped her forehead. "You know how to reach me if you want to meet up before next week's scheduled afternoon here."

The newest Tomorrow Person then jaunted home.

Megabyte extracted his hand from Ami's, giving her a sideways look. "Okay," he said. "That was weird."

"I wanted to stop you just going before we had a chance to talk."

"Could've just said 'Hey Megabyte, don't shoot off yet' rather than... that. Whatever that was."

Ami patted the seat next to her. "Sit."

"Yes Mom."

For a second no one said anything. Then finally Ami spoke.

"That was a hell of a gift you got Adam for his birthday last night."

If Megabyte, whose hair and freckles were always pretty flame-coloured, could have got redder in the face, well, it would have been difficult.

"Just seemed... nice," he finally said.

Another few seconds of silence. Then Ami reached forward and eased Megabyte's embarrassed face round so they were looking one another in the eyes. "When are you going to tell him?"

Megabyte squirmed and pulled away slightly, but Ami didn't let go. "Tell who what?" he asked.

Ami sighed. "You know exactly what I'm talking about. Pretty sure Jade would if she were here." Ami then smiled. "Kevin and Lisa, less so. I don't think

47

they notice anything other than each other right now."

Megabyte said nothing for a second, then yanked his head out of Ami's grip and stood up. "Look, I don't know what you are talking about, Ami, but just drop it."

"I'm trying to help," she said quietly.

"I... I just don't know what you mean," he repeated.

"But I..."

Megabyte then did something Ami had rarely seen before. He flared up, and shouted at her. "Whatever is going on in your head," he yelled, "don't bring me into it, okay?"

Ami blew air out her cheeks. "Okay. But Megabyte... Marmaduke... I'm here if and when you want or need to talk about it. Because it's not going to go away."

Megabyte said nothing but just jaunted out of the Ship.

Ami closed her eyes, annoyed with herself and concerned for her friend.

Friends.

This was not going to end well. When people didn't talk about things that mattered, it never did.

Outside, Megabyte was sat on the beach, looking out across the Pacific Ocean. He remembered that first time he'd been unceremoniously dumped in the water when teleporting in. Meeting Kev's new friends Lisa and Adam. Later Ami and Jade. Showing his dad his new powers and how they could benefit everyone.

Over the past few years, Megabyte could see they all grown up, changed, not just puberty-style changes but mentally. They had different attitudes, different wants and needs to those rather young and foolish kids who'd started this... Ami would say "this great adventure", Jade would say "this utter madness". Right now, he wasn't sure which of them was closest to the mark.

He'd told his dad so many of his secrets—hell, his dad had been here to the island more than once. There weren't many secrets he could keep from him now.

Not many.

Of course he *knew* exactly what Ami was talking about just now. He wished he didn't, he wished... oh he wished so many things. Mostly that the noise in his head about it all would shut up. It was so much easier when they all first met, had fun, fought the bad guys, saved the world.

But whatever else had happened, Megabyte had developed… no, no it didn't matter. Because it wasn't going to change.

"Wish human brains came with instruction manuals," he muttered, throwing a handful of sand into the water. "Actually, wish I could just rewrite that manual, and put everything back the way it was."

"Hey man, what's up?"

Megabyte froze.

Had he heard what he'd just said?

He felt Adam's hand grasp his shoulder. Just as it had many times over the years. They were mates, they'd always had that easy familiarity, that closeness, that…

Megabyte shrugged his shoulder, causing Adam's hand to come lose.

Why? Why had he done that? What good was that going to do?

Adam sat beside him. "Thank you again for the photo of Dad." Adam looked at him, that slight cock of his head, that grin that went from his mouth up into his eyes, that flick of his hair, that…

"You will not believe the weirdness of what I just escaped from. The old folks threw a party for me—guess Lucy told them—but then this weird old woman turned up. Not seen her before."

"Was Lucy there?"

"No, I mean really old," Adam laughed. "She won't thank you for that by the way," he added.

Adam reached in and nudged Megabyte's shoulder and—

"Don't! Just... don't."

Megabyte jaunted away, leaving Adam alone.

Megabyte's bedroom was the bedroom of a kid. He hated it. As he stood there, fresh from the island, Megabyte realised that he'd not changed a picture or poster or anything since becoming a Tomorrow Person.

He had grown up. His room hadn't.

God, he still called himself Megabyte, a nickname Mom had given him nearly ten years ago.

Mind you, it was still marginally better than Marmaduke.

Maybe he could call himself Duke going forward.

Nah, sounded like an old cat.

He smiled wryly as he thought that if he had Ami's powers, he could wave a hand and rip everything off the walls, scoop it all up in some kind of freaky psychic wind force and chuck it out the window.

Instead he had to manually pull the posters down.

Seattle bands no one in the UK had heard of. Movie posters from films now in Blockbuster's £1 bin. There was a small magazine-sized illustrative poster of a Japanese girl in a sailor suit from some video game. She had blonde pigtails, chibi eyes and unfeasibly large breasts that in real life would have "caused her to fall over", according to Dad, when he'd seen it.

Megabyte had been so embarrassed. His dad had been in his room, looking at his posters.

He'd also commented on how pretty the girl was. Megabyte had mumbled some kind of agreement.

What had he been thinking? Who had he been trying to fool? Dad? Mom? Himself?

As the posters came down, as the action figures got put way, as the kids bedroom became... bland, a small photograph dropped down to the floor.

It had been taken about a year ago, outside the front door.

Adam had been wearing that amazing orange sweater that seemed two sizes too big and always smelled of fresh soap. Megabyte had been in a tight white T shirt that was probably two sizes too small. Adam's arms had been round Megabyte, almost cuddling him.

Megabyte noticed that in the photo he was leaning back against Adam, almost pushing himself into that hug.

Dad had taken it and given him the print a few days later.

Did he know? Had he seen what Megabyte hadn't? Or hadn't wanted to. Was this his way of starting a conversation that had never happened?

No. Course not. To Dad it was just two mates hanging out.

He needed to talk to Dad. See him. Say hi. He'd got so used to teleporting in and straight out of the house via the bedroom, he barely went downstairs anymore. It'd probably been days since he and Dad had said anything longer than "hi" or "How's Adam?"

Never "How's Ami?". Or Jade. Mind you never "How's Kevin?" either—and Megabyte and Kevin had been friends far, far longer than anyone else.

Megabyte left his room and started the walk down the steps.

Dad was standing in the hallway, by the kitchen door. Staring into space, probably thinking about some secret service thing.

"Hey, Dad," Megabyte said. "You okay?"

General Damon said nothing.

Megabyte got close to him, reached out, touched his shoulder.

General Damon didn't move a muscle. Megabyte stood in front of him, realising that his father was completely out of it. He waved a hand in front of his closed eyes. "Hey, old man, wake up," he laughed.

Nothing.

Had he had a stroke? A heart attack? Megabyte looked at the phone, call 999 he thought.

The phone line was very obviously cut.

This was serious, this was an attack. Who was the target though. Dad or him?

If it had been Dad, he'd be on the floor, dead or something.

Megabyte had been doing this long enough. His dad wasn't dead, there was a pulse and everything. He was in some weird trance, waiting for Megabyte to find him.

Megabyte clenched his fists, and they glowed slightly red. "Ami," he said telepathically.

"Hey," was her immediate response.

"Something's wrong with Dad."

"Hospital wrong or Tomorrow People wrong?"

Megabyte actually stifled a smile. Yeah, they'd all been doing this long enough. "Us wrong." The something struck him. "When did you last speak to your mum?"

Silence.

Megabyte stayed staring at his dad. He spotted that his eyes were moving, like he'd seen on TV, when people are dreaming, and their eyes move weirdly under the eyelids. REM sleep he thought it was called.

So his dad was conscious, in a way, dreaming something.

A flash and electricity and Ami was beside him. She looked at General Damon.

"Mum's the same."

"Go look at her eyes," Megabyte said.

Ami vanished. Then reappeared. "Mum's the same as that too."

"Then they are alive and, zombie stance aside, presumably okay."

"A message? To us? From who?"

Megabyte couldn't answer that, but he had one other thought.

"Jade?"

55

Jade Weston lived in the countryside, far away from the city of London. Although her time with Adam, Ami and everyone had meant she'd spent a lot of time in the city, and a few others around the country, she was at heart, a country girl.

Her mum, Penny, lived in a nice village called Mulberry, and although it had once been invaded by extra-terrestrials and everyone had had their minds dominated and forced into nearly destroying planet Earth, it was a pretty nice place.

Jade and her mum had a nice cottage which they shared with their dogs Bonny and Jester and relatively recently, a cat called Pegleg, because it only had one eye. No Jade didn't understand that either, but she and her mum had just accepted this—Pegleg had come to live with them after old Ms Triplett had finally passed away and calling a one-eyed cat Pegleg was very in keeping with Ms Triplett's eccentricities.

Pegleg had been checked over by Ruth Tanner, the vet from Boscown, the nearby 'big town' (it wasn't much bigger than Mulberry, but had a hospital, a railway station and a nightclub, so it automatically became the 'big town' to all the satellite villages round).

Jade had known Ruth for years—but had got to become really close friends recently as her nephew was Kevin Wilson, one of Jade's fellow Tomorrow People. Jade wanted to be a vet when she was younger so had spent a lot of time with Ruth, which had made her becoming a Tomorrow Person that much easier as Ruth had gone through it with Kevin—and according to Kevin, dealt with it far more reasonably than his actual parents had.

All that said, Jade still made a point of teleporting in, jaunting as Adam called it, in a secluded part of one of the fields near Mulberry itself. The last thing she wanted to do was alert any of the neighbours to her powers. Being taken over by alien rocks, *that* they could deal with. But a telepathic, teleporting teenager who could also read their moods and temperaments, oh no, that was never going to be an acceptable part of village life.

By the time Jade had walked to her home, it was getting dark.

As she opened the gate, she expected to hear Bonny and Jester barking to greet her.

Nothing.

That was odd. Mum's car was there, so she'd not taken them anywhere and it was unlikely that she'd be walking them this close to dinnertime.

The hairs on Jade's neck stood up.

She looked down at her hands and concentrated. Her hands glowed slightly, a faint red light and she called out with her mind to Adam.

No reply.

Ami.

No reply.

Megabyte.

No reply.

It was like something was blocking her powers. She let her telepathy fade and walked hurriedly up to the front door.

It was open.

That was very unlike her mum.

She reached out and put her hand on the back door—and a second later she was standing, frozen staring ahead.

Her eyes were closed but moving rapidly, seeing something no one else could.

Adam was inside the Ship. He'd heard Megabyte's call in his head, but it had been a call for Ami, not him.

Which was odd. But then Megabyte was being odd these days.

What was he missing? Megabyte had never been like this before? Yesterday it had been all smiles and laughs and the birthday photo gift. Today, he was like a grumpy teenager. Ha, Adam thought, it reminded him of when he'd broken things off with Lucy and she'd been all hostile for a few days.

Adam sighed. As a kid, people had always said he was a bit standoffish, a bit unapproachable. Adam thought that was weird, he was behaving quite normally, but some people just wanted his attention, his... space, if you like... a bit too much.

"Just like your father," his mum had said to him once. "You're both somewhere on the spectrum."

Adam had been too young to understand what that meant back then; now he did and, although he reckoned his mum had meant it as an insult, Adam took it as a huge compliment. Who wanted to be just like everyone else anyway?

But that was his mum. When he was young, he hadn't really understood her attitude, her problem. Now, of course, he could look back and see how alcohol dependent she was, and possibly other stuff too.

Charlotte Newman had been a lady in need of help but, rather than face and accept it, she'd run away and Adam had never seen her again.

Perhaps he ought to try and track her down. Chances were, she had returned to England. Maybe Megabyte's dad could help. Mind you, that'd involve asking Megabyte for help and clearly, right now, Adam had done something to upset him, and Adam hadn't got a clue what.

Thinking about his mum had brought something else up in Adam. He thought about that photograph Megabyte had given him and he wandered to one of the recessed areas of the Ship, where he kept his personal stuff.

Ami, Megabyte, Jade, they all had homes to go to where their lives were. Kev and Lisa the same.

But since the day he'd first washed up on the shore of this island, the island that somehow he knew he'd been searching for on the horizon the day he said goodbye to his dad's ashes on Avoca Beach, Adam hadn't had a home.

So the island, the Ship especially, had become his refuge. He wasn't particularly proprietorial about it, but the amount of time he spent here meant he had some kind of rapport with the intelligence that ran it. Ami asked him once if he could understand the burbles and rumbles the Ship made. No, he couldn't, not in a language sense. But something stirred inside him when it made those noises and he certainly understood the Ship's intent, if not the actual words. There was something primeval about the Ship. And primal. He felt comforted by it, like he knew it was protecting him.

As a result, his entire worldly belongings were stored here. A quick midnight teleport to Mart's place one night enabled him to shove everything he wanted into a couple of bags and he was gone.

He'd gone back a night later and left Mart a note—it wasn't fair to just disappear without a word, but he made it clear he wasn't coming back.

He hoped Mart understood.

Adam opened up a box of stuff. Ticket stubs from train journeys he'd taken with his dad. A toy car he'd got for his fifth birthday. Some papers (including his birth certificate, Adam had made sure he got that). There was even an out of date passport—one of the joys of jaunting was that you didn't really need to worry about passports and visas and stuff any longer.

It crossed Adam's mind what would he do if all his powers vanished? What if Tomorrow People hit, say twenty-one, and their powers vanished, they became the Yesterday People?

Cross that bridge when you come to it, mate, he told himself.

His eye was drawn to a small square of card. On one side, a London Underground symbol, on the other a name.

John Dixon.

Adam had often thought about the Englishman on the beach all those years ago. He'd always meant to ask Red Rainwear if he had been one of his group, like the tall schoolboy or the guy with the tortoise. But he hadn't seen sight nor sound of Red Rainwear's people for a couple of years now.

Adam dropped the card to the floor, not deliberately, but in surprise.

Facing him across the Ship was the old woman from the Mission House that morning, complete with her shopping trolley.

Adam had been doing all this long enough to know that asking her how she got there was silly. The fact that she was there, in the Ship, in the South Pacific and not North London, implied she was more powerful and dangerous than he had ever imagined.

"Who are you exactly?" was the most obvious thing he could say.

"Not 'how did you get here?' Oh that is a shame."

Adam shrugged. "You *are* here. And it's a long way from London, so I'm guessing you probably didn't walk."

"Smartarse," she said.

"Lottie Oldham, wasn't it?"

"It's the name I go by in this little slice of human history, yes. I've used quite a few before." Lottie paused. "You didn't like your mum very much, did you?"

"I didn't really know her," Adam said, thinking that was an odd question. "Do you know her?"

"She's dead."

Adam tried not to show that this was a punch to the gut. He swallowed and said, almost too quickly, "How do you know that?"

He knew the answer before Lottie spoke. The nasty, almost rictus grin on her face told him what he needed to know. "I'm afraid poor Charlotte Newman-nee-Dell died so that I might live. I needed someone connected to you and genetically she was the best choice, your father having chosen to annoy me by dying a few years earlier."

"You knew my dad too?"

"He was my son, Adam. I'm your little old paternal Grannie."

"An orphan and a grandmother all in five minutes," Adam countered. "What a day for revelations."

Lottie giggled. "You are so like your father. He was flip and arrogant and hid everything underneath humour too." Her demeanour changed, her voice deepened, almost angrily. "I spent thousands of years trying to find him, throughout time. And just as I got there, people like you stopped me."

"People like me?" Adam hadn't a clue what she was talking about but keeping her talking seemed a better way of finding out rather than shutting up or jaunting away.

"They called themselves the Tomorrow People. Like you, they had powers. Slightly different ones of course, some stronger than yours, some weaker. Each generation skips and plays with the genes."

"Was my dad a Tomorrow Person?"

"Oh yes, a very special one. He was the First. Well, okay, actually I was probably the *real* first one, but he was the first to use his powers. Thousands of years ago, in a cave, somewhere in Africa. I tried to kill him, thinking I could get that power for myself, but I failed. Again thanks to modern day Tomorrow People. Time travel you see. Sort of. Temporal projection, really. Your dad's fault.

Again. Now he's gone, I'm going to take all that power from you. And then Ami. And Megabyte. And Jade. And Kevin. And Lisa. Oh, and probably a number of other people dotted around the world." She laughed again. "You don't think the group of you are *it*, do you? Oh this century has coughed up more Tomorrow People than you can shake a stick at. Some, like you lot, gather together. Others keep themselves to themselves. Then there's you. Adam Newman. May I say what an arrogant name Joshua took for himself: 'new man' indeed—did you know the word 'Neanderthal' is derived from the German for 'new man'? Anyway, you have his DNA. The most powerful *homo superior* DNA of them all. An actual living breathing *homo novus*. And my plan is to keep myself alive for a few thousand more years, by stripping that DNA out of you and absorbing it into myself, molecule by molecule."

"That doesn't sound like fun. For me, anyway."

"Oh it won't be. It will hurt you Adam, as you die. Rest assured, I'll enjoy causing that pain so *very* much."

Megabyte swore, really quite loudly. And then a second time.

"Ami," he said telepathically. "Jade's here. Just like my dad and your mum. Frozen."

Megabyte stepped past Jade and looked into the house. "Penny's the same. So are Jester and Bonny. Weird. Just staring."

Ami was suddenly beside him in a crackle of bio-electrical disturbance.

"This is not good," she said. "Really not good."

"You think?" Megabyte snapped, more harshly than he probably intended. "Look, someone's out to get us," he added, a bit more softly.

"You sure it's us?"

"I don't see any non-TPs frozen, do you? I reckon it's just us and our families."

Ami nodded. "But why leave them here, like statues. Where people can find them?"

Megabyte shrugged. Then a thought struck him. "Where we can find them. It's a calling card."

"Eh?"

"Seriously, think about it. Your mom. My dad. But Jade's mom *and* Jade."

"And the dogs."

"Yeah and the dogs. But why freeze Jade but not you or I?"

66

Ami nodded as she got what he was saying. "It's us. You, me and probably Adam. But not the others."

"I mean, sure I like being someone's favourite Tomorrow Person," Megabyte muttered, crouching down to the frozen dogs. "But not like this."

"We need to warn Adam."

Megabyte grunted something under his breath, and Ami kicked his bum. "Not now," she said sternly. "This is too serious to let whatever's going in in your head—and his—get in the way. Come on, back to the Ship."

They both jaunted home.

The Ship was in complete darkness as they arrived, the tiny vestige of their bio-electrical jaunting only illuminating it for a split-second.

"This can't be good," Ami said.

"No," Megabyte agreed. He blinked a couple of times, trying to get his eyes adjusted quicker. It didn't work.

Ami suddenly knelt down and told Megabyte to join her.

"Why?"

"Just place your hand on top of mine. Think healing thoughts."

"I'm not a healer," Megabyte protested. "That's His Royal Highness King Adam's speciality. I'm just like a slight booster when he needs juicing up."

"Me too," Ami said. "Maybe two boosters can give out enough to help the Ship wake up."

They placed their hands on the Ship's floor— frankly Megabyte felt silly and said so.

Even through the dark, Megabyte could imagine the look he was getting from Ami. "Got any better ideas?"

"No," he said. "I actually think it's a neat idea. I also don't think it'll work, but let's give it a go."

A second later, a slight greeny-yellow glow from their combined powers flowed through their hands into the floor of the Ship.

Three or four seconds later, the central column of the ship started to glow in response; its usual cobalt-blue, although only at ten per cent of normal, was enough to show Megabyte and Ami what they needed to see.

Hovering in mid-air, to the right of the column was Adam. Unconscious, just... hanging there as if on an invisible meat hook.

Megabyte gasped and felt Ami squeeze his hand. Megabyte just stared at Adam, emotions washing over him, unbidden and annoying.

Concern.

Panic.

Confusion.

And lo—

"Hullo, you must be Marmaduke Damon. Oh and Ami Harris, how marvellous."

They both turned to face an elderly woman opening up a canvas shopping trolley.

"How the hell did you get in here?" Megabyte demanded.

"Oh, same way as you. Quantum superposition, with a bit of localised warping of the air. All those molecules being kicked about, they get all excited and angry and create all that smelly electricity. Luckily, I snuck in without that cos, well, I've been doing this a long time."

"What do you want?" asked Ami.

"A sensible question at last. Power, my young friends. Power and survival. Which I'm starting to get from my grandson here. And you two as the Tomorrow People running up the most frequent flyer points on using your powers over the last few years, will be dessert."

"Just who are you?"

"Call me Lottie Oldham."

Megabyte frowned, that name was familiar... He'd seen it on an ad somewhere, back home... "Hang on, the vet woman?"

"Fame at last," Lottie cackled. Then she snarled. "What are you doing, young lady?"

Megabyte could see Ami had dropped to the floor, and she was feeling around, claiming some scattered bits and pieces. A passport, some scraps of paper, the photo Megabyte had given Adam of his dead father.

Her hand was reaching for a small rectangular card, like a business card.

Ami scooped it up and Megabyte could just make out in the dim light that on one side was a London Underground logo, no station name on the blue bar. Flipping it over, he saw that a single name had been written there but he couldn't see what.

Weird.

"Megabyte, have you ever seen anything like this before?" Ami opened her mouth to say something else but her body simply vanished.

Lottie grunted angrily. "Now, where has Miss Jackson gone, I wonder?"

"Let Adam go," Megabyte spat.

She just laughed. "Oh bless but no, I don't think so. Grannie needs him exactly as he is right now. In the meantime, young man, I have someone to introduce you too."

She reached into her shopping trolley and brought out something that caused Megabyte to let out a loud yell of fear.

He flopped to the floor, like someone had switched his body off. In his last seconds of consciousness, he stared at a tentacled creature that was now on the floor before him, reaching towards his head...

Episode Three

SECONDS LATER...

Ami wasn't sure what shocked her most; the fact that she was inside a strange place she'd never seen the likes of before, or the fact that there were people in it, staring at her in exactly the same amount of shock.

The place reminded Ami of a disco. A bad disco. A bad school disco. One of those discos that, after the rise of house music, had decorated itself in retro 1970s tech.

Or tack.

The most notable thing was some kind of circular giant lava lamp hanging down from the ceiling, all oils and patterns flowing through it rhythmically. Below it was an up-lit coffee table.

Around the edges of the disco (surely also the smallest as well as the tackiest disco ever) were a series of indented seating areas, with big cushions.

Somehow Ami sensed she was underground and, although much smaller than the Ship, it somehow reminded her of that. Maybe it was the soft, almost imperceptible hum, or that nice sweet smell that the Ship always gave out which was similar to the atmosphere in here. Where here was.

"We call it the Lab," a voice said inside her head. Male, authoritative but calm. Calming even. Okay, that was telepathic, Ami knew. She looked at the four people still staring at her, open-mouthed in surprise.

Only two guys, and she guessed neither of them had spoken to her.

"My name is TIM," said the voice and Ami realised it wasn't telepathic any more. This was being spoken aloud. The people gathered there all looked up to the giant inverted lava lamp-thing in the ceiling. "You are most welcome, Ami."

"Thank you," she found herself saying. "Where am I? Where are you?"

"I am all around you," the voice, this TIM, said. "But my main focal point is the biomorphic matrix you are looking at above the table."

Ami realised the lava lamp-like patterns were rolling and pulsating as TIM spoke. Whatever he was, he was inside that... thing.

"TIM's a computer," said a tall dark-haired man—mid-forties Ami guessed—in a white polo-neck sweater. He held out a hand. "May I have a quick look at the calling card that brought you here?"

Utterly bewildered, Ami robotically handed it over.

"I'm John," the man said.

The name written on that card was John Dixon. Surely that had to be him?

Ami looked at him again. He was smiling. So now were the three other people.

Firstly there was the other guy, late twenties probably, flame-haired a bit like Megabyte, and wearing a kilt (which Megabyte would never have the kahunas to pull off wearing). He had a cheeky grin and a twinkle in his eye, and Ami relaxed a little.

Next to him was a younger Indian girl, probably fourteen or fifteen. She was in jeans and a Haçienda T-shirt and had a bindi on her forehead.

Standing by what Ami assumed was a door (why couldn't she have come through that instead of teleporting in?) was possibly the most beautiful woman she'd ever seen. Her poise, her bone structure, her whole affect suggested she was some kind of Asian goddess. The three-piece business suit she wore off-set that slightly, but Ami guessed she was a woman used to being in charge.

The older man, John passed the card to the young Indian girl. "Neena, can you get a reading from this?"

The younger man nudged Neena. "See, told you the practice would pay off."

"Thanks, Andrew," Neena said as she closed her eyes, holding her hand a few centimetres above the card. A faint green glow seemed to come from her palm.

She then stopped and passed it back to John.

"I can read your trace on it, John, but from a long time ago. You gave it to someone on a beach, I think. But warm, so not a British beach. America or... no, Australia I think." She nodded. "Its biometrics are keyed for a boy, called... I can't get the name, sorry. It's been halfway round the world and not exactly well-taken care of."

John nodded. "Brilliant, Neena. Well done!"

Andrew nudged Neena. "All down to my excellent tuition, of course."

"Oh, of course," Neena said back.

John meanwhile looked up at the pulsating blobs in the computer above. "TIM, if I recall, the boy was called Adam. I can picture him, yes, at his father's wake."

"Newman," Ami added in the missing information. "Adam Newman."

"His father was Joshua Newman, TIM. That's why I went."

Ami coughed. "Look, this is great and everything, but can I just ask something myself now? Like where am I? And why?"

"We call ourselves the Tomorrow People, Ami," said Andrew.

"So do we," she replied slightly sharper than she'd intended. *It's not a competition, Ami,* she mentally chided herself.

"Fascinating," TIM the computer said. "Parallel groups of Tomorrow People, unaware of one another but based here in London. Do you have a Lab like this, Ami?"

Ami shook her head. "Our base isn't even in England."

"Scotland?" asked Andrew.

"No, our base is somewhere in the South Pacific. It's an island. We… teleport there. Adam calls it jaunting."

"So do we," said the austere Asian lady by the door. Ami wasn't sure from her tone if she found it fascinating, like TIM did, or deeply annoying that they shared the word.

"My name is Hsui Tai," she said, bowing slightly. "I have been working with John and TIM for many years now."

"Me too," Andrew added. "But Neena here only broke out a few months back, so this is still new to her."

"Broke out?"

"Yeah," Andrew said, still smiling. He smiled a lot. Ami quite liked that in him. "That moment where you go from being a Sap to a Tomorrow Person."

If Ami was about to wonder aloud what 'Sap' meant, TIM cut in. "Ami, I sense you didn't jaunt into the lab here deliberately. May I ask what is going on? Does it involve Adam Newman?"

Ami nodded. Then added "Yes TIM," in case he couldn't see her. "Something is going on." She sighed. "Adam is our leader. There's this old woman after him. She's done something to people's brains, shut them off. Including my mum."

"I'm sorry to hear that," John said. "Are you okay?"

Ami nodded again. "Yeah. Yeah I'm fine, par for the course in our line of work. She's got Megabyte's dad, my mum, plus Jade's mum. We haven't heard from Lisa or Kevin in America, so we don't know if she's taken any of their family but Adam and I reckon not."

"Why do you think that?"

"Because Lisa would be back to the Ship in a second if anything happened to her folks."

Andrew frowned. "Ship? You live on a spaceship?"

"No," Ami said. "Our Ship is… a bit like this place I suppose. It's even a similar layout. But it's under an island in the South Pacific. It's… alive, a bit like you, TIM, but can't talk. Well, not to the rest of us, but Adam seems to have some kind of rudimentary way of getting through to it. Jade thinks it's more empathy than telepathy and… and…" Ami stopped. "I'm talking too much, aren't I?"

"Not at all, Ami," said TIM. "Indeed, I find the Ship fascinating. It makes a lot of sense."

"How do you mean, TIM?" asked John.

"We know some things from the Galactic Trig records," TIM carried on. "Possibly millions of years ago, certainly tens of thousands of years ago, beings of great power roamed the universe. It is said they were telepathic, almost Godlike in their powers."

"The Kultan?"

"Even older than them, John. We do know from records on a number of planets that they owned sentient star ships, using a technology we can only dream of. It has long been suspected, assumed even, that the reason Tomorrow People broke out on Earth in the first place was because these people, and possibly their ships, arrived here at some point."

"You think our Ship is one of theirs?" asked Ami.

"It is only supposition, Ami. But the fact your Ship is under an island, in the South Pacific, an area of great change during the continental drifts, would certainly make it a possibility. John, you may not recall but when the Trig first suggested this spot to build the Lab, it was in a pre-existing space."

"Yes," John said, "but an old disused tube station, so we wouldn't be disturbed."

Ami now understood the tube logo on the calling card.

TIM was carrying on. "Yes, but one of the reasons the Lab works so well, and why constructing me was so easy within this space, may be because the Lab was possibly built on the site where one of those Ships landed and had then been destroyed over the aeons."

"Excuse me," Ami piped up. "History lessons are great in school but I came to you because Adam is in trouble. This old woman, Lottie Oldham she called herself, has him and has hurt him badly I think."

"Who exactly is this she?" Neena asked.

Ami shrugged. "I don't know. Adam certainly didn't know her either. But she claims she's his grandmother!"

"John," TIM said slowly. "I have had a thought about this woman. Adam's grandmother. Which makes her…"

John's eyes widened. He looked at Ami, and she was sure there was fear in his face now. "Ami, do you have any photos of this grandmother?"

"Course not."

"Ami," TIM said soothingly. "May I, only with your permission of course, probe your memory? If you can picture her, I can retrieve it, show it on our screen. And you can confirm I have the right image."

Ami frowned. "You can rummage around in my head?"

"I can," TIM said. "But I absolutely will not without your full consent."

"But it could be important," John cajoled, but quite kindly.

"Sure," Ami said. "Have a look."

Ami felt absolutely nothing, TIM was that good. But she gasped when on a screen on the far side of the room, near Andrew and Neena, a really very clear image of Lottie Oldham appeared.

"Is that her?" Hsui Tai asked.

"Absolutely is."

"So, we knew Joshua Newman had a son, Adam. Josh was the very first Tomorrow Person." John shook his head. "It's not the same face, but there's something in those eyes. I know it's her."

"Who?" asked Hsui Tai.

"TIM and I knew a similar woman, twenty years ago, as Juniper Rose. Josh's mother and therefore Adam's grandmother." John looked at Ami. "What Adam probably didn't know is that his father was born in Neanderthal times and lived through history, his mother one step behind, always trying to destroy him. She nearly destroyed me over twenty years back."

Ami tried to take this in. "Adam's related to… a caveman?"

"We assumed we had stopped her permanently," TIM explained. "John, it seems we were wrong."

Ami was staring into space, trying to get her head wrapped around all this. "And his grannie is a cavewoman? This is mad."

John scooped up a jacket and slipped it on. "Ami, I need to come with you if that's all right?"

Ami nodded. What else could she do?

"Us too," Andrew said, but John spoke quickly and quietly. "No, Andrew. You and Hsui Tai need to stay here, protect TIM, the lab and Neena. This woman is dangerous. This is something I have to do alone. Or rather, alone apart from Adam's generation of Tomorrow People." He smiled at Ami again. "Can we go to this Ship of yours please? TIM—stay in touch at all times, I... we *all* may need you."

Ami took John's hand and in a crackle of electrical energy, they both jaunted out of the Lab...

...and appeared in the Ship.

Facing them was Lottie Oldham, sitting on a seat, eating a mango, canvas shopping trolley beside her.

"That's her," Ami told John.

Lottie stood up, a grin spreading across her face, eyes fixed on Ami's new friend.

"John Dixon," she breathed out. "Well, that I did *not* expect." She threw a glance towards Ami. "I suspect, dear girl, you've heard the phrase killing two birds with one stone? Well, if John's here, that gives me the chance to kill two species with one plan! How utterly delicious. Thank you."

Out of the corner of her eye, Ami saw something scuttling over the floor and, in a moment of ludicrousness, she thought it looked a bit like an octopus.

Ami's last thought was that everything had gone a bit wrong.

Then she was unconscious.

In a dark part of the Ship, Adam and Megabyte were tied crudely, but very efficiently and tightly, to a couple of chairs that Adam recognised as coming from the old people's Mission House in London. They were placed back to back, tied with the same bit of rope.

Adam wriggled, trying to see if he could loosen the rope, but Lottie Oldham had tied them very well indeed.

"Could you stop?" asked Megabyte angrily.

"Stop what?"

"Moving around like that. Every time you do, these ropes cut into my wrists."

"We should try teleporting away. Jaunt outside to the beach or—"

"Oh," Megabyte replied. "Oh yeah, cos that had never occurred to me before you woke up. I just sat here, waiting for Adam Newman to save me." Megabyte then sighed. "We can't teleport. That creature, the thing with all the tentacles, it did something to my head, I can't think about teleporting. Or focus on what I normally do to make it happen."

Adam focussed but nothing happened. "Me too. Some kind of mental block," he blew air out of his cheeks. "That's impressive."

"Glad you're happy," snorted Megabyte.

Adam flared up, because he was over this. "Look, what the hell is wrong with you at the moment? I mean, what have I done?"

"Nothing."

Adam sighed. "You mean nothing is wrong with you or I've done nothing?"

Megabyte swallowed. Loudly. "Both. Neither. I don't know."

Adam was getting cross now. "Look, mate, you and I have been doing this for years now. We always had each other's backs. I trusted you, you trusted me. But now… now I don't know if I can do that. And I don't know what's changed."

Silence.

Adam sighed. He didn't know whether to punch Megabyte or walk away from him. Not that there was any way he could do either right now. Plus jaunting away wasn't possible thanks to Lottie's little spell, besides Adam was getting increasingly frustrated by Megabyte's attitude. Out of character attitude, too.

"I... I like you."

Three words, said so quietly Adam almost didn't hear them, his brain sort of pieced together the noises and translated them into what he assumed Megabyte said.

"Good," he relied with a sigh. "Although you have a funny way of showing it. For the record, I still like you too."

"No," Megabyte snapped suddenly. "I like you. I... *like* you..."

Adam frowned. What was he talking about now.

Then it hit him.

The amazing photo gift for his birthday.

Ami's weird comments.

The recent distance between him and Megabyte.

That angry exchange on the beach.

And... Megabyte's standoffishness with Lucy for all those months.

Those odd moments of anger when Adam had gone off on adventures with Jade or Kevin or...

Jealousy?

However, "Define 'like me'," was all Adam heard himself say. Instantly wishing he hadn't. He wished he could say something else.

"I..." Megabyte went silent again.

Adam was cross because Lottie had placed them back-to-back. He couldn't see Megabyte. Couldn't look at his friend. "You know I'm straight, right?" Adam muttered, and again instantly wanted to kick himself. Because *of course* Megabyte knew that and it so wasn't the thing to say to him right now.

"I know," Megabyte said. "But I... Forget it. I'm sorry."

Adam finally leaned back, so the back of his head was on Megabyte's shoulder. Gently, carefully. Affectionately.

"Don't you dare be sorry," he said to Megabyte. "*I'm* sorry. I'm sorry I hadn't realised. I'm sorry I hadn't stopped to see how this was hurting you. Sorry most of all that I can't be what you want, what you need me to be. But hell, man, I'm your mate. Your *best* mate. That can't change. It won't change. And for that I am really, really sorry."

Megabyte shrugged Adam's head off his shoulder,

but not angrily. Just sort of deflated. Adam could almost sense the air sagging out of his American mate as he lifted his head.

"If I could," Megabyte finally said, "I'd use whatever Tomorrow People powers I have to reach into my heart, flick off whatever switch must be in there, anything to stop feeling this way about... about you. But I..."

"You can't," Adam prompted "And you shouldn't. It's what makes you tick, mate. Thank you for telling me. It changes nothing."

"It changes *everything*," Megabyte countered. "Because I just said all that out loud. God, I just told the person... the *man*... I'm in love with that I love him. And all I can think about is how that affects the rest of my life. Dad. Mom. They'll hate me as much as you do."

Adam tried to turn to look at Megabyte—he really wanted to see his best mate's face right now. "I don't hate you. I couldn't hate you if you paid me. And c'mon, you know the General. He accepted your powers, aliens... hell, your red hair. He'll accept this without blinking, because he loves you." Adam gave Megabyte's shoulder another nudge with his head. "And I'll be there when you tell him if you want me to be."

"Why?"

"Because *that's* what this friend is for, okay?"

Ami awoke to find herself curled up on the floor, her hands evidently tied behind her back.

She rotated around and managed to right herself, so she was at least sitting upright. Her head felt... weird.

"Hullo, Ami."

She glanced to her left. John Dixon was there, similar predicament.

"I can't jaunt," he said rather plaintively. "Our friend Juniper Rose or Lottie or whoever she really is, she did something to my head."

Ami frowned. "I'm the same," she finally confessed.

John seemed to sag a bit more. "This is not good," he muttered. "I can't raise TIM or anyone telepathically either."

"She's done a number on all of us," said a familiar voice, and Ami was instantly pleased to see Megabyte being pushed towards her by Lottie Oldham.

"I'm John. You must be Megabyte."

Megabyte nodded.

"Where's Adam?" Ami asked.

"Enough questions," Lottie said, forcing Megabyte to his knees next to the others.

Her creature with the tentacles loomed out of the darkness, followed by Adam. But Lottie didn't send him to join his friends. Instead, she almost dragged him close to the Ship's central column. "That explains our loss of powers," John said darkly.

"What, the octopus?" asked Megabyte.

"It's a Medusa. Specially bred to drain our powers. Both telepathy, and everything else. How did she get one?"

"Pet shop? She is a vet."

"I think John's suggesting it's not from Earth," Ami said.

"I was trying not to think along those lines," Megabyte said.

"Adam?" Ami hissed across the Ship, but he just gave her a sad look. "I think she's won," Adam said plainly, a sound of defeat and misery in his voice Ami hadn't heard before.

She didn't believe it for second. Because Adam was never defeatist.

"TIM," Andrew snapped, as he paced the Lab, "why can't I contact John?"

"I do not know, Andrew," the computer answered, and even Neena could sense the slight panic in TIM's normally calm voice.

She looked across at Hsui Tai, whose hands were already palm down on the table, using it to boost her telepathy. "John," she said. "John, can you hear me?"

"It's no good," Andrew said. "He's out of range."

"If John was out of range of me," TIM said, "he would have to be on one of the outer planets of the galaxy. Otherwise, using the Trig's equipment, I at least would be able to sense him."

"What are you saying?" Neena asked. "That's he's dead?"

Both Andrew and Hsui Tai gave her look that suggested that not only was that an unacceptable question, but it was an outcome they simply weren't prepared to countenance.

"I hope not, Neena," TIM said. "The most likely other option is that he and our new friend Ami have been attacked by someone using something

90

Medusan. Nothing else can stop our thoughts getting through on even the smallest level."

Lottie Oldham was striding around the Ship. Adam was standing immobile next to its central column, which pulsated slowly and far less vibrantly than normal. This was probably due to the presence of Lottie's pet Medusa which had a tentacle wrapped round Adam's ankle.

"So," Lottie addressed Ami, Megabyte and John, like some eccentric schoolmarm. "Allow me to explain a few things." She patted the Ship's wall. "Somewhere in the region of one hundred and thirty thousand years ago, something came to Earth. It was a representative, almost an ambassador, from one of the universe's eldest species. No one on Earth knew anything about this—they were still ghastly ignorant primitive pygmies, halfway between *homo heidelbergensis* and *homo neanderthalensis*."

"Anyone else bored yet?" asked Megabyte.

Lottie ignored him. "These aliens were a powerful race who existed generally as beings of pure thought—physical form was repugnant to them, they had moved beyond that when the universe was still new. But they were benign and kindly, they saw the universe as a crucible for them, a chance to bestow their morality and ethics onto the universe at large. They would find species with the genetic possibilities to be peace-loving, intelligent, sophisticated creatures and guide them. Usually this only applied to about 0.4% of a planetary population, but that was enough for them."

"Of course they didn't come themselves, no, they sent their ships; living, breathing organic craft controlled by a living mind. These ships would arrive on a planet in its early stages, settle there and wait patiently for the species to evolve to a point where that 0.4% could be contacted. And show them how to help their own people, their own worlds. The ultimate good Samaritans really. Such tedious and pointless ideals to have."

"TIM had a theory," John said. "TIM thinks one of those ships landed on Earth, here in the South Pacific. Of course, the land mass it landed on was probably soft, maybe even molten and the ship dipped below the surface and this island formed around it, yes?"

Lottie gave him a short clap of applause.

"Periodically, it would send out a signal, a beacon, see if anything advanced enough would recognise it."

"Adam?" suggested Ami.

"Ha, no. Well, yes in the end, but he wasn't the first, not by a long way. But I was. I was young then, but I heard its call and made my way across seas and lands, very different to the topography you have today, but I got here. Took me years. By the time I found the ship, this Ship—just in case you missed the point because for all your arrogance, you Tomorrow People are pretty dim—I was, well, knackered. Dying really."

Lottie crossed back to her grandson, stroking a long finger down his cheek in mock affection. "But the Ship let me in. It spoke to me, just as it speaks to you, Adam. Do you know why it let you in?"

"No, go on, tell me."

"Because I'm your grandmother. It saw in you the same genetic perfection that it saw in me. And all those hundreds of thousands of years ago, it woke my mind, it showed me what I could be. But because I didn't have exactly the same Tomorrow People strand of mutant DNA that you lot have, my power really just became..."

"Immortality?" suggested John.

93

"No," Lottie said. "Not quite. But certainly a very, very long life. And I'd really quite like to carry on living. Hence all this." She waved her hand towards the four of them. "You and all the other Tomorrow People across this planet, ones you know, ones you don't, I'm going to rid you all of that genetic anomaly and absorb it into myself, via Adam here as our DNA is pretty intertwined already. That should give me another two or three hundred thousand years."

"What have you done to Jade?" asked Megabyte. "And my dad, Ami's mom and so on?"

"They were the carrots, they were what I needed to get you three here and now. The more powerful of Adam's gang. Would you like me to release them? And all the others I hold in thrall?" She looked at Adam. "All those wretched, smelly, rancid coffin-dodgers at the Mission House you frequent so often?"

Megabyte growled. "Yes. Release my dad now."

"Please?"

"Please," he added darkly.

"Pretty please? With sugar and honey and—"

"Juniper Rose!" John snapped. "Or Lottie or whatever you are calling yourself this decade, those Saps have done nothing to hurt you. Release them."

94

Lottie leaned in conspiratorially towards Megabyte and Ami. "John here gave me a bit of a lecture about twenty years ago about the value of 'family'. At the same time *he* was turning mine against me, but then hypocrisy has always been a hallmark of John Dixon."

"You mean my dad?" Adam said quietly from behind her.

Lottie nodded. "I was pretending to be a medium, and they brought Joshua to this time. Like me, he had a long lifespan, the one thing he inherited from me I imagine. But he was also a full-on Tomorrow Person. I was going to absorb him, but they put an end to that. Just think, Adam, if they hadn't, you'd never have been born and your Ship here would have lain unfound for centuries more."

"You're a sponge," John said.

Lottie laughed and pointed to the Medusa, still latched to Adam's leg. "I think my little pet would be insulted to hear you use that word like it's something unpleasant."

"Sponges have limits…" John said, and Ami saw that he aimed that squarely at Adam.

"Where did you find it?" Ami asked, hoping to distract Lottie while Adam and John were exchanging what she assumed were meaningful looks.

"When you've lived as many centuries as I have, young lady, you meet all sorts of people from other worlds paying a visit. I think it was some trader, or pirate, or thief. I honestly can't recall. Mister Medusa and I have been a team for quite some time now."

Lottie beeped Megabyte on the nose. "Daddy is free and awake now. Same as Ami's mumsie-wumsie and all the others. See, Adam, I can be nice."

"How do we know you are telling the truth?" snapped John.

"You don't," Lottie laughed. "But I don't need... what is it you so derogatorily call them John? Oh yes 'Saps'. I don't need Saps and frankly, I could do without the Medusa expending the energy on them."

"What now?" Adam asked.

Lottie walked up to him and kissed his forehead. "Now my little kith and kin, it's time to say goodbye."

At which point the Medusa let go of Adam and wrapped itself around the base of the Ship's central column.

The Ship gave out what Ami could only think of as a scream of utter pain.

Then, with shock, she realised Adam was screaming in unison.

General Bill Damon found himself stood at the foot of his stairs. He took a deep breath. Whatever had been going on was finished.

"Megabyte," he breathed. Somehow he knew his son and Ami had been there, in the house with him, at some point.

But where were they now?

Adam ignored the pain as best he could, focussing instead on what really mattered right now.

John had referred to his grandmother as a sponge, trying to absorb his, everybody's, powers. But John, who had so much more experience with her, had asked Adam what happened when a sponge exceeds its limits to take on water.

It absorbs so much but eventually it can't hold on and it overflows. It ceases to hold its shape, its strength. Ultimately it just becomes a very wet, useless lump of polyester.

Adam smiled and caught John's eye, relieved to see the older man relax slightly. They'd understood what the other was thinking, even though they couldn't telepathically link.

Consciously.

But unconsciously, he clearly had. On some level John had suggested a... plan was probably too strong a word right now, but... intent. Idea. No, "plan" would do, actually.

"Feed me, Adam Newman," purred Lottie. "Feed me all of their powers, all of that glorious *homo superior* DNA, *homo novus* genetics."

Sure, Adam thought. *If that's what you really want, Grannie.*

"Oh Adam," she said in his ear. "You are the locus I never imagined you could be. Everything your father was, and so much more." She threw a glance at her Medusa, sat patiently by the central column of the Ship. "See my darlings? Lottie told you we'd win."

Adam just smiled. Lottie had no idea what she had unlocked in him.

Invisible to the naked eye, invisible to everyone except Adam, a thin tendril of pulsating and rotating light shot out from his forehead and straight into John's.

Another tendril into Ami.

A third into Megabyte (forgive me for this, he thought).

All three of them went rigid and their eyes glowed pure white.

"Yes," Lottie said, and Adam could feel her drawing the power back out of him. He was like a battery, connected to the other Tomorrow People, and simultaneously feeding all that energy back into his grandmother.

"Boost him!" Lottie shrieked in delight. "Yes, boost him *now*."

Jade was sat with her mum, drinking tea and playing with the dogs when her eyes suddenly glowed white and, unseen by her mum, but quite possibly by the dogs because animals pick up on things humans can't, a tendril of pulsating, rotating light shot out of her forehead, up and over the trees and fields, across the British Isles and out across the world towards the South Pacific.

At a fairground in Shakopee, Kevin and Lisa were wandering arm in arm, both enjoying some cotton candy when their minds turned off, their eyes glowed white and an invisible tendril shot out from both of them, up into the sky and then across to the Pacific Ocean...

In the Lab, TIM tried getting a response from Andrew, Hsui Tai and Neena, but no one returned his cries. TIM could sense, via his biometrics, the tendrils of psychic energy being leeched from his young charges.

In a south London travel agency, a girl called Elena Plowright stopped writing out a customer's holiday request, as her eyes went white, and an invisible tendril shot out of her head.

In an unassuming Ministry of Defence building in Shropshire, Tricia Conway dropped the box-files she had been carrying, her eyes glowing white, a tendril of power raging out of her forehead.

In the caravan that Tyso and Evergreen Boswell had inherited from their parents a couple of years back, the two siblings were hosting a games night with Stephen Jameson and Debbie Crossland. D12 dice, character sheets and pencils dropped to the floor as the four of them had their Tomorrow People energy sapped out of them via tendrils of light from their foreheads.

On a farm in Northumberland, the owners— fraternal twins Cynthia and Adrian Price—stood in a field. They were ignoring, or unaware, of the rain pelting down upon them as tendrils threaded out of their foreheads.

Hasana Jackson was sitting in her kitchen, making a cup of coffee for her sister.

"Your niece is giving me endless headaches," she was saying. "Ever since she got involved with Adam and Megabyte, I'm really scared that something bad is going to happen. I mean, I know Ami's not a chid any more but…"

Hasana stopped talking. Because her sister clearly wasn't listening. Instead, she was sat at the kitchen table, immobile, her eyes blazing with white energy.

"Elisabeth?" Hasana said. "Elisabeth, can you hear me? Are you alright?"

Ten minutes before going on stage at the Labatt's Apollo in Hammersmith, the Fresh Hearts' lead guitarist couldn't raise drummer and singer Mike Bell from within his locked dressing room.

In outer space, on the Galactic Trig, Ambassador Kenny Green stood in his quarters, staring down at planet Earth through sightless white eyes, a tendril of power leeching from his forehead down towards his homeworld. Elsewhere on the same Federation base, Ambassador Carol MacNeil-Tran and her Andonesian husband Narcissa and their sons Nova and Lukis were operating the Overmind Projector when their own telepathic powers similarly linked them with Adam, leaving them all white-eyed and static.

All these tendrils of pulsating light were roaring into Adam's own head, but he was smiling as it did so, still ignoring the pain and instead enjoying the overwhelming energy filling up his body. Like a sponge.

Beside him, Lottie Oldham placed her fingers on his temples and gasped, feeling the energy within him. "Yes," she breathed. "Finally, my birthright. Aeons of waiting has come to this, immortality, no more endings and beginnings, no more finding new bodies and lives to weave." She took a deep breath. "I'm almost sorry, Adam. The family line finally ends here with you. But that's life." She laughed. "Or death."

Then Lottie frowned, because against all the odds, Adam's own hands reached up and pulled hers away from his head.

Adam stood up, his eyes burning white hot. Lottie had to turn away slightly, the brightness was almost too much to bear.

The central column of the Ship lit up equally brightly and Lottie could see five, ten, no dozens of tendrils of light pouring into it, coming from... outside.

Somehow.

Lottie tried to break Adam's grip but it was supernaturally strong and she could see his hands were glowing white too.

Behind him, the three other Tomorrow People raised their own hands in a weird, puppet-like manner, echoing Adam's movement.

From out of the glowing column of the ship a massive concentrated beam of light, focussing all the individual tendrils coming from Tomorrow People all over the world, and beyond, into one massive beam into Adam. Within seconds, Lottie could no longer see anything other than Adam, the whiteness had blotted out everything else. The Ship, the Tomorrow People, her Medusa, even Adam was just a silhouette to her now.

"You wanted my... our power, Grannie," said his voice deep within her mind. "Have it with pleasure."

"I... I can't... I can't absorb it all..." Lottie gasped. "No, you can't give me all that..."

"I'm not giving anything," Adam said. "It's you. You're taking the energy from a dozen, a hundred, maybe a thousand Tomorrow People. I don't honestly know. But if you don't quit this, get away from me and my friends, I can't stop you absorbing all this."

"I can control it," Lottie shrieked. "And I damn well won't be stopped by some ungrateful snotty-nosed off-spring of my own disappointing, ungrateful child. I will destroy you, Adam, you and all of them."

"Are you sure?"

"I was the First Tomorrow Person ever. And when you are destroyed, I will be the Last. And best."

"Please don't do this, Lottie. Grannie. Grandmother. You are all the family I have left. We could—"

Lottie snarled and spat in his face. "Family? You are no more family to me than a blade of grass or a bumble bee is."

"I'm sorry," Adam whispered.

Then the brightness within the Ship flared one last time and everything went back to normal.

Megabyte was on his knees. He wasn't sure how he got there, but it had to do with something Adam had done to him just now. Or an hour ago. Or was it days? Megabyte realised he had no idea.

He reached out to steady Ami, who was lying face down but shakily trying to get up.

"Look." That was the new guy, John.

Megabyte looked.

Adam was standing there, facing Lottie Oldham. She was literally pulsating with power—white light crackling around her and her whole body seemed to be translucent. Megabyte couldn't see anything organic inside her, but her body seemed to be moving slightly, changing shape every few seconds, and the power within her was fluctuating madly.

"Should we get away?" Ami asked. "Is it safe to be here?"

"I don't know," said John. "But I do know the Medusa is still stopping us jaunting."

"I just want to sleep," Ami said.

Any further discussion was interrupted by the old woman. "I will destroy you all!" she growled.

"No you won't," replied Adam. Dead calm. Utterly unafraid.

Megabyte had never felt prouder of him.

"Lottie," Adam said quietly. "I want you to be calm, be relaxed. Stop all this."

"Never!"

Adam sighed. "Listen to my voice. Think of Joshua, your son. Think of me, your grandson. Think of that power within you. Imagine sharing it rather than devouring it, hoarding it." Adam reached a hand out but she slapped it away. He offered it again, imploringly. "I want you to imagine that your mind is a fist, Lottie. A great big fist. Clenched tight. Now, let it open, slowly. Don't let any other thoughts come into your head. Just think of the fist opening very slowly, like the petals on a flower. Now imagine that flower. And a foetus, birthing. Stars. Galaxies. Shadows and shapes. Seeds. Earth. Fire. Water. Air. The fist opening and closing."

"If I can't have your powers, your genetics, your lives, then I will destroy you all," she spat in return.

"I can't let that happen," Adam said. "The Ship won't let that happen. It has waited an eternity for us to be here. Please, don't anger it."

"It's just a machine," Lottie hissed.

The 'machine" gave another sound, but this time it was the Medusa creature that responded, by promptly going 'pop' into a thousand pieces of dead jelly.

"You monster!" Lottie screeched at the Ship. "You utter—"

Megabyte then heard a sound he had never heard before, and never wanted to again. It was a scream so primal it seemed to vibrate right through him.

Slowly, inch by inch, Lottie Oldham seemed to start... unwinding was his best description. Like layers of her just detached and vanished into smoke.

She was reaching out for Adam's throat, but her hand never got there. It became wisps, followed by her arm and within a few seconds, Lottie was gone, as if she had never even been there.

Adam just stood, staring at the space where his grandmother had been.

"First my dad. Then my mum. And now this. I only knew her for a couple of hours... but she was all I had."

Megabyte forced himself up, forced himself to cross the space between them and then threw himself around Adam, holding him tightly.

"I'm so sorry," he said. "So so sorry."

Adam turned to face Megabyte and then buried his head into Megabyte's shoulder, trying not to sob. And failing, frankly.

After a few seconds, he looked up into Megabyte's face. "Megabyte, you have to get away from me."

It was like a punch to the gut for Megabyte, delivered by a large number of trucks. And a wrecking ball in full swing. "Why?" he asked.

"Seriously, mate," Adam said. "All that energy, it went back into me when she ceased to exist. I'm going to do the same way any second. I can feel it. And I can't let it kill you too."

"I'm not going anywhere." He smiled at Adam. "Because that's what *this* friend is for."

Adam almost smiled back but instead eased

himself away from Megabyte. "You're the best. Goodbye."

Megabyte couldn't believe this. Couldn't accept he was going to lose the most important person in the universe. Okay, so Adam didn't feel the same way and yeah, he always knew that, deep down.

But he wasn't prepared to say goodbye.

"Ship," Megabyte yelled. "You can't let Adam die."

The tell-tale dull echoey sound of the Ship reverberated around, as if it was agreeing with Megabyte.

"Hey, it answered you," Adam coughed. Hugging himself, as if that would help keep the energy inside from leaking out. "Look after it."

"Adam."

The Ship, after so many years, finally spoke aloud. In English. "Adam," it repeated. "Trust me."

Adam Newman vanished. No explosion, no burst of energy like that which had destroyed Lottie Oldham, no lights or pyrotechnics. He just wasn't there any longer.

"Did he jaunt?" John wondered aloud.

As if in answer, the whole room was flooded once again with the white light.

Then it was gone.

Megabyte felt better, stronger than he had in a while.

Ami was beside him now. "The Ship," she said. "It's returned our energy back to us. I feel fantastic."

"Hopefully that's true for everyone else around the world," said John. "And beyond."

"What happened to the old woman?" Ami asked.

"Adam did his best to convince her to stop absorbing us," John said. "But everything has a breaking point. She simply obliterated herself by taking on more than she could absorb."

"Like a bag full of too much water…" Megabyte reasoned.

"Or a sponge," said a voice behind them.

Megabyte didn't need to turn round. He knew that voice to the core of his heart.

He felt Adam's arm round his shoulder and saw the other one snake around Ami's.

"The Ship saved us all," Adam said.

"Where did you go?" asked John.

Adam shrugged. "I'm not really sure. Somehow, I think I was inside the Ship, just for a few moments. Enough for him to get everything out of me and back into… everyone else." Megabyte finally allowed himself to turn and see Adam's smile.

Adam kissed Ami's cheek and ruffled Megabyte's hair. "You don't get rid of me that quickly, guys."

"What now?" asked Ami.

"We do what we do best," Adam said.

"What's that?" asked Megabyte.

"We throw a bloody great party."

The party was in full swing. It was on top of the hill at Alexandra Palace in North London. Adam stood slightly apart from everyone, not because he was feeling antisocial, but because there were a lot of people and it was overwhelming trying to remember the names and faces.

Ami was there with her mum and her auntie Elisabeth, who bizarrely John Dixon knew. Small world.

Jade and Penny were there, along with Bill Damon, catching up with Kevin and Lisa, plus a couple of John's Tomorrow People friends. Andrew and Neena he thought they were called.

A girl calling herself Evergreen—and they all thought Megabyte was a weird name—had come over at one point and told him she'd heard a report that a lot of old age pensioners in North London had told the police that they'd been kept prisoner in some Mission House.

"Cool," he said. "I'll check in on them soon, make sure they're all okay."

John was talking to a blonde lady who apparently was some bigwig from outer space called Carol and a couple of guys—Stephen and Tyso were the names that popped into his mind.

Adam gave up trying to recall everyone else's names. That would happen in time. It seemed insane for two separate Tomorrow People groups to stay separate forever, and whilst Adam was pretty sure he preferred his island and his Ship to a claustrophobic London Underground lab, the offers to come and go to one another's bases had been made and accepted.

Ami wandered over, can of cola in hand, which he took gratefully.

"How're you doing, boss man?"

Adam smiled. "I'm okay, thanks."

"And truthfully?"

"I miss him. I thought he'd show up with his dad, but I guess not." He looked at Ami "How did you know, and I didn't?"

Ami shrugged. "Woman's intuition. Plus I could see the signs. You two have a pretty weirdly close friendship, very tactile, very buddy/buddy. It's no stretch for one of you to fall for the other."

"You could have told me. Warned me."

"Not my right. Megabyte's his own man."

There was silence for a few seconds.

"It was really brave of him to tell you. Not sure he'd even told himself at that point."

"It was a… situation that presented itself, I guess." Adam sighed. "I wish I could talk to him."

"What's stopping you?"

"Cos I don't know where he is."

Ami rolled her eyes. "I've said it before, I'll say it again. You are a complete moron." She jabbed Adam's forehead. "Where d'you think he is?"

Adam frowned. He really didn't… oh.

"Finally," Ami said, heading back to the party. "See you later."

Megabyte was sat on the beach, looking out across the Pacific Ocean.

"Room for one more?" asked Adam.

"It's a big beach, buddy."

Adam sat down.

After a few seconds, they both looked at one another.

"I'm sorry," they said, simultaneously. And then laughed.

"Talked to my dad."

"What did he say?"

"Exactly what you said. Something about aliens, teleporting around the world, this place and then hugged me. I cried. He cried." Megabyte nodded slowly. "Yeah, he's fine and actually really cool."

"Told your mum?"

"Told Millie."

"Ahh, same thing then."

"Yup, she'll love that. At school she'll be dead popular. 'I got a gay brother,' she'll say. That'll make her top of the cheerleader squad in no time."

Adam smiled. "I can imagine."

Pause. A long pause. Then:

"What happens now, Megabyte?"

"I dunno. I'd love to say nothing changes, we carry on as always, put it all aside. But…"

"But you can't. As you said, you can't just turn it off. I'm sorry. Again."

Megabyte turned back to stare at the sea. "If I stay here, right now, it'll mess with my head. Every time I look at you, instead of fighting the bad guys, or getting your stupid ass out of whatever stupid fire you put it in, as usual, I'll be thinking 'why couldn't it be different?'. And in an emergency, that's no good to either of us. Or Ami. Or Jade or anyone else."

"So?"

"I'm going to stay with Mom, Stateside, for a while. Dad's okay with that, he gets it."

"No one ever said being a Tomorrow Person was easy."

"Ain't that the truth." Megabyte shrugged. "But I'll be back, that's a promise. When I'm ready. When I can… deal."

"I'm going to miss you," Adam said. "But I get it. I'll do my best to make sure we don't meet any aliens or mad world dominating old ladies or… nah, who am I kidding?"

Megabyte laughed. Then he reached sideways, without taking his eyes off the sea and grasped Adam's hand. "I need my best mate in my life. You get that, don't you."

Adam squeezed it back. "He's not going anywhere. There's a whole new generation of Tomorrow People out there, according to John. I need you to come back and help train them."

"I love you, Adam Newman."

"Love you too. Mar-ma-duke."

Megabyte shook his head. "Man, you are evil."

"Sure am. Mar-ma-duke."

"Give everyone else my love." Megabyte let go of Adam's hand and stood up. He still didn't, maybe couldn't, look Adam in the eye. "See you round, bud."

Then Adam was alone on the beach.

Just as he had been all those years before, when he first wound up there, his first ever jaunt.

When his life as a Tomorrow Person had first begun.

When he'd first found home.

ROGER PRICE'S

THE

TOMORROW PEOPLE

SEASON TWO

GARY RUSSELL

COLIN BRAKE

GEORGE IVANOFF

KENTON HALL

IAIN McLAUGHLIN

REBECCA LEVENE & DAVID DERBYSHIRE

SEPTEMBER 2025